The Magic City

*Three days later Mr. Noah arrived by elephant.*

# The Magic City

✧ E. NESBIT ✧

WITH ILLUSTRATIONS BY H. R. MILLAR

AFTERWORD BY PETER GLASSMAN

BOOKS OF WONDER

*SeaStar Books*

NEW YORK

SEASTAR BOOKS
a division of NORTH-SOUTH BOOKS, INC., New York

Published in the United States by SeaStar Books, a division of
North-South Books, Inc., New York. Published simultaneously in Canada,
Australia, and New Zealand by North-South Books, an imprint
of Nord-Süd Verlag AG, Gossau Zürich, Switzerland.
Nord-Süd Verlag has made every good faith effort to locate the
appropriate rights holder and to obtain permission to publish
the illustrations contained in this book.

Library of Congress Cataloging-in-Publication Data
Nesbit, E. (Edith), 1858-1924.
The magic city/by E. Nesbit; jacket illustration by Paul O. Zelinsky;
interior illustrations by H. R. Millar.
p.   cm.
Summary: An extremely unhappy ten-year-old magically escapes into a
city he has built out of books, chessmen, candlesticks, and other household items.
[1. Fantasy.] I. Millar, H. R., ill. II. Title.
PZ7.N437877 Mag 2000    [Fic]—dc21    00-25204

ISBN 1-58717-024-8 (trade binding)
1  3  5  7  9  TB  10  8  6  4  2

ISBN 1-58717-025-6 (paperback)
1  3  5  7  9  PB  10  8  6  4  2

PRINTED IN THE UNITED STATES OF AMERICA

Books of Wonder is a registered trademark of Ozma, Inc.

For more information about our books,
and the authors and artists who create them,
visit our web site: www.northsouth.com

*To*

*Barbara, Maurice,*

*and*

*Stephen Chant*

THIS BOOK IS DEDICATED

BY

E. NESBIT

✧

WELL HALL,
ELTHAM, KENT 1910

# Contents

# Illustrations

The Magic City

# CHAPTER ONE

## The Beginning

PHILIP HALDANE and his sister lived in a little red-roofed house in a little red-roofed town. They had a little garden and a little balcony, and a little stable with a little pony in it—and a little cart for the pony to draw; a little canary hung in a little cage in the little bow window, and the neat little servant kept everything as bright and clean as a little new pin.

Philip had no one but his sister, and she had no one but Philip. Their parents were dead, and Helen, who was twenty years older than Philip and was really his half sister, was all the mother he had ever known. And he had never envied other boys their mothers, because Helen was so kind and clever and dear. She gave up almost all her time to him; she taught him all the lessons he learned; she played with him, inventing the most wonderful new games and adventures. So that every morning when Philip woke he knew that he was waking to a new day of joyous and interesting happenings. And this went on till Philip was ten years old, and he had no least shadow of a doubt that it would go on forever. The beginning of the change came one day when he and Helen had gone for a picnic to the wood where the waterfall was, and as they were driving back behind the stout old pony, who was so good and quiet that Philip was allowed to drive it. They were coming up the last lane before the turning where their house was, and Helen said, "Tomorrow we'll weed the aster bed and have tea in the garden."

"Jolly," said Philip, and they turned the corner and came in sight of their white little garden gate. And a man was coming out of it—a man who was not one of the friends they both knew. He turned and came to meet them. Helen put her hand on the reins—a thing which she had always taught Philip was never done—and the pony stopped. The man, who was, as Philip put it to himself, "tall and tweedy," came across in front of the pony's nose and stood close by the wheel on the side where Helen sat. She shook hands with him, and said, "How do you do?" in quite the usual way. But after that they whispered. Whispered! And Philip knew how rude it is to whisper because Helen had often told him this. He heard one or two words, "at last," and "over now," and "this evening, then."

After that Helen said, "This is my brother, Philip," and the man shook hands with him—across Helen, another thing which Philip knew was not manners, and said, "I hope we shall be the best of friends." Pip said, "How do you do?" because that is the polite thing to say. But inside himself he said, "I don't want to be friends with *you*."

Then the man took off his hat and walked away, and Philip and his sister went home. She seemed different, somehow, and he was sent to bed a little earlier than usual, but he could not go to sleep for a long time, because he heard the front doorbell ring and afterward a man's voice and Helen's going on and on in the little drawing room under the room which was his bedroom. He went to sleep at last, and when he woke up in the morning it was raining, and the sky was gray and miserable. He lost his collar stud, he tore one of his stockings as he pulled it on, he pinched his finger in the door, and he dropped his toothmug, with water in it too, and the mug was broken and the water went into his boots. There are mornings, you know, when things happen like that. This was one of them.

Then he went down to breakfast, which tasted not quite so nice as usual. He was late, of course. The bacon fat was growing gray with waiting for him, as Helen said, in the cheerful voice that had always said all the things he liked best to hear. But Philip didn't smile. It did not seem the sort of morning for smiling, and the gray rain beat against the window.

After breakfast Helen said, "Tea in the garden is indefinitely postponed, and it's too wet for lessons."

That was one of her charming ideas—that wet days should not be made worse by lessons.

"What shall we do?" she said. "Shall we talk about the island? Shall I make another map of it? And put in all the gardens and fountains and swings?"

The island was a favorite play. Somewhere in the warm seas where palm trees are, and rainbow-colored sands, the island was said to be—their own island, beautified by their fancy with everything they liked and wanted, and Philip was never tired of talking about it. There were times when he almost believed that the island was real. He was king of the island and Helen was queen, and no one else was to be allowed on it. Only these two.

But this morning even the thought of the island failed to charm. Philip straggled away to the window and looked out dismally at the soaked lawn and the dripping laburnum trees, and the row of raindrops hanging fat and full on the iron gate.

"What is it, Pippin?" Helen asked. "Don't tell me you're going to have horrid measles, or red-hot scarlet fever, or noisy whooping cough."

She came across and laid her hand on his forehead.

"Why, you're quite hot, boy of my heart. Tell sister, what is it?"

"*You* tell *me*," said Philip slowly.

"Tell you what, Pip?"

"You think you ought to bear it alone, like in books, and be noble and all that. But you *must* tell me; you promised you'd never have any secrets from me, Helen, you know you did."

Helen put her arm around him and said nothing. And from her silence Pip drew the most desperate and harrowing conclusions. The silence lasted. The rain gurgled in the water pipe and dripped on the ivy. The canary in the green cage that hung in the window put its head on one side and tweaked a seed husk out into Philip's face, then twittered defiantly. But his sister said nothing.

"Don't," said Philip suddenly, "don't break it to me; tell me straight out."

"Tell you what?" she said again.

"What is it?" he said. "*I* know how these unforetold misfortunes happen. Someone always comes—and then it's broken to the family."

"*What* is?" she asked.

"The misfortune," said Philip breathlessly. "Oh, Helen, I'm not a baby. Do tell me! Have we lost our money in a burst bank? Or is the landlord going to put bailiffs into our furniture? Or are we going to be falsely accused about forgery, or being burglars?"

All the books Philip had ever read worked together in his mind to produce these melancholy suggestions. Helen laughed, and instantly felt a stiffening withdrawal of her brother from her arm.

"No, no, my Pippin, dear," she made haste to say. "Nothing horrid like that has happened."

"Then what is it?" he asked, with a growing impatience that felt like a wolf gnawing inside him.

"I didn't want to tell you all in a hurry like this," she said anxiously, "but don't you worry, my boy of boys. It's something that makes me very happy. I hope it will you too."

He swung round in the circling of her arm and looked at her with sudden ecstasy.

"Oh, Helen, dear—I know! Someone has left you a hundred thousand pounds a year—someone you once opened a railway-carriage door for—and now I can have a pony of my very own to ride. Can't I?"

"Yes," said Helen slowly, "you can have a pony; but nobody's left me anything. Look here, my Pippin," she added, very quickly, "don't

4

ask any more questions. I'll tell you. When I was quite little like you I had a dear friend I used to play with all day long, and when we grew up we were friends still. He lived quite near us. And then he married someone else. And then the someone died. And now he wants me to marry him. And he's got lots of horses and a beautiful house and park," she added.

"And where shall I be?" he asked.

"With me, of course, wherever I am."

"It won't be just us two any more, though," said Philip, "and you said it should be, forever and ever."

"But I didn't know then, Pip, dear. He's been wanting me so long—"

"Don't *I* want you?" said Pip to himself.

"And he's got a little girl that you'll like so to play with," she went on. "Her name's Lucy, and she's just a year younger than you. And you'll be the greatest friends with her. And you'll both have ponies to ride, and—"

"I hate her," cried Philip, very loud, "and I hate him, and I hate their beastly ponies. And I hate *you*!" And with these dreadful words he flung off her arm and rushed out of the room, banging the door after him—on purpose.

Well, she found him in the boot cupboard, among the gaiters and galoshes and cricket-stumps and old rackets, and they kissed and cried and hugged each other, and he said he was sorry he had been naughty. But in his heart that was the only thing he was sorry for. He was sorry that he had made Helen unhappy. He still hated "that man," and most of all he hated Lucy.

He had to be polite to that man. His sister was very fond of that man, and this made Philip hate him still more, while at the same time it made him careful not to show how he hated him. Also it made him feel that hating that man was not quite fair to his sister, whom he loved. But there were no feelings of that kind to come in the way of the detestation he felt for Lucy. Helen had told him that Lucy had fair hair and wore it in two plaits; and he pictured her to himself as a fat, stumpy little girl, exactly like the little girl in the story of "The Sugar Bread" in the old oblong "Shock-Headed Peter" book that had belonged to Helen when she was little.

Helen was quite happy. She divided her love between the boy she loved and the man she was going to marry, and she believed that they were both as happy as she was. The man, whose name was Peter Graham, was happy enough; the boy, who was Philip, was amused—for she kept him so—but under the amusement he was miserable.

And the wedding day came and went. And Philip traveled on a very hot afternoon by strange trains and a strange carriage to a strange house, where he was welcomed by a strange nurse and—Lucy.

"You won't mind going to stay at Peter's beautiful house without me, will you, dear?" Helen had asked. "Everyone will be kind to you, and you'll have Lucy to play with."

And Philip said he didn't mind. What else could he say, without being naughty and making Helen cry again?

Lucy was not a bit like the Sugar Bread child. She had fair hair, it is true, and it was plaited in two braids, but they were very long and straight; she herself was long and lean and had a freckled face and bright, jolly eyes.

"I'm so glad you've come," she said, meeting him on the steps of the most beautiful house he had ever seen. "We can play all sort of things now that you can't play when you're only one. I'm an only child," she added, with a sort of melancholy pride. Then she laughed. "Only rhymes with lonely, doesn't it?" she said.

"I don't know," said Philip, with deliberate falseness, for he knew quite well.

He said no more.

Lucy tried two or three other beginnings of conversation, but Philip contradicted everything she said.

"I'm afraid he's very very stupid," she said to her nurse, an extremely trained nurse, who firmly agreed with her. And when her aunt came to see her the next day, Lucy said that the little new boy was stupid, and disagreeable as well as stupid, and Philip confirmed this opinion of his behavior to such a degree that the aunt, who was young and affectionate, had Lucy's clothes packed at once and carried her off for a few days' visit.

So Philip and the nurse were left at the Grange. There was nobody else in the house but servants. And now Philip began to know what loneliness meant. The letters and the picture postcards which his sister sent every day from the odd towns on the continent of Europe, which she visited on her honeymoon, did not cheer the boy. They merely exasperated him, reminding him of the time when she was all his own, and was too near to him to need to send him postcards and letters.

The extremely trained nurse, who wore a gray uniform and white cap and apron, disapproved of Philip to the depths of her well-disciplined nature. "Cantankerous little pig," she called him to herself.

To the housekeeper she said, "He is an unusually difficult and disagreeable child. I should imagine that his education has been much neglected. He wants a tight hand."

She did not use a tight hand to him, however. She treated him with an indifference more annoying than tyranny. He had immense liberty of a desolate, empty sort. The great house was his to go to and fro in. But he was not allowed to touch anything in it. The garden was his—to wander through, but he must not pluck flowers or fruit. He had no lessons, it is true; but, then, he had no games either. There was a nursery, but he was not imprisoned in it—was not even encouraged to spend his time there. He was sent out for walks, and alone, for the park was large and safe. And the nursery was the room of all that great house that attracted him most, for it was full of toys of the most fascinating kind. A rocking horse as big as a pony, the finest dollhouse you ever saw, boxes of tea things, boxes of bricks—both the wooden and the terra-cotta sorts—puzzle maps, dominoes, chessmen, draughts, every kind of toy or game that you have ever had or ever wished to have.

And Pip was not allowed to play with any of them.

"You mustn't touch anything, if you please," the nurse said, with that icy politeness which goes with a uniform. "The toys are Miss Lucy's. No; I couldn't be responsible for giving you permission to play with them. No; I couldn't think of troubling Miss Lucy by writing to ask her if you may play with them. No; I couldn't take upon myself to give you Miss Lucy's address."

For Philip's boredom and his desire had humbled him even to the asking for this.

For two whole days he lived at the Grange, hating it and everyone in it; for the servants took their cue from the nurse, and the child felt that in the whole house he had not a friend. Somehow he had got the idea firmly in his head that this was a time when Helen was not to be bothered about anything; so he wrote to her that he was quite well, thank you, and the park was very pretty and Lucy had lots of nice toys. He felt very brave and noble, and like a martyr. And he set his teeth to bear it all. It was like spending a few days at the dentist's.

And then suddenly everything changed. The nurse got a telegram. A brother who had been thought to be drowned at sea had abruptly come home. She must go to see him. "If it costs me the situation," she said to the housekeeper, who answered:

"Oh, well—go, then. I'll be responsible for the boy—sulky little brat."

And the nurse went. In a happy bustle she packed her boxes and went. At the last moment Philip, on the doorstep watching her climb into the dogcart, suddenly sprang forward.

"Oh, Nurse!" he cried, blundering against the almost moving wheel, and it was the first time he had called her by any name. "Nurse, do—do say I may take Lucy's toys to play with; it *is* so lonely here. I may, mayn't I? I may take them?"

Perhaps the nurse's heart was softened by her own happiness and the thought of the brother who was not drowned. Perhaps she was only in such a hurry that she did not know what she was saying. At any rate, when Philip said for the third time, "May I take them?" she hastily answered:

"Bless the child! Take anything you like. Mind the wheel, for goodness' sake. Good-bye, everybody!" She waved her hand to the servants assembled at the top of the wide steps, and was whirled off to joyous reunion with the undrowned brother.

Philip drew a deep breath of satisfaction, went straight up to the nursery, took out all the toys, and examined every single one of them. It took him all the afternoon.

The next day he looked at all the things again and longed to make something with them. He was accustomed to the joy that comes of making things. He and Helen had built many a city for the dream island out of his own two boxes of bricks and certain other things in the house—her Japanese cabinet, the dominoes and chessmen, cardboard boxes, books, the lids of kettles and teapots. But they had never had enough bricks. Lucy had enough bricks for anything.

He began to build a city on the nursery table. But to build with bricks alone is poor work when you have been used to building with all sorts of other things.

"It looks like a factory," said Philip discontentedly. He swept the building down and replaced the bricks in their different boxes.

"There must be something downstairs that would come in useful," he told himself, "and she did say, 'Take what you like.'"

By armfuls, two and three at a time, he carried down the boxes of bricks and the boxes of blocks, the draughts, the chessmen, and the box of dominoes. He took them into the long drawing room where the crystal chandeliers were, and the chairs covered in brown holland—and the many long, light windows, and the cabinets and tables covered with the most interesting things.

He cleared a big writing table of such useless and unimportant objects as blotting pad, silver inkstand, and red-backed books, and there was a clear space for his city.

He began to build.

A bronze Egyptian god on a black and gold cabinet seemed to be looking at him from across the room.

"All right," said Philip. "I'll build you a temple. You wait a bit."

The bronze god waited and the temple grew, and two silver candlesticks, topped by chessmen, served admirably as pillars for the portico. He made a journey to the nursery to fetch the Noah's Ark animals—the pair of elephants, each standing on a brick, flanked the entrance. It looked splendid, like an Assyrian temple in the pictures Helen had shown him. But the bricks, wherever he built with them alone, looked mean, and like factories or workhouses. Bricks alone always do.

Philip explored again. He found the library. He made several journeys. He brought up twenty-seven volumes bound in white vellum with marbled boards, a set of Shakespeare, ten volumes in green morocco. These made pillars and cloisters, dark, mysterious, and attractive. More Noah's Ark animals added an Egyptian-looking finish to the building.

"Lor', ain't it pretty!" said the parlor maid, who came to call him to tea. "You are clever with your fingers, Master Philip, I will say that for you. But you'll catch it, taking all them things."

"That gray nurse said I might," said Philip, "and it doesn't hurt things building with them. My sister and I always did it at home," he added, looking confidingly at the parlor maid. She had praised his building. And it was the first time he had mentioned his sister to anyone in that house.

"Well, it's as good as a peep show," said the parlor maid. "It's just like them picture postcards my brother in India sends me. All them pillars and domes and things—and the animals too. I don't know how you fare to think of such things, that I don't."

Praise is sweet. He slipped his hand into that of the parlor maid as they went down the wide stairs to the hall, where tea awaited him—a very little tray on a very big, dark table.

"He's not half a bad child," said Susan at her tea in the servants'

*"Lor', ain't it pretty!" said the parlor maid.*

quarters. "That nurse frightened him out of his little wits with her prim ways, you may depend. He's civil enough if you speak him civil."

"But Miss Lucy didn't frighten him, I suppose," said the cook, "and look how he behaved to her."

"Well, he's quiet enough, anyhow. You don't hear a breath of him from morning till night," said the upper housemaid, "seems silly-like to me.

"You slip in and look what he's been building, that's all," Susan told them. "You won't call him silly then. India an' pagodas ain't in it."

They did slip in, all of them, when Philip had gone to bed. The building had progressed, though it was not finished.

"I shan't touch a thing," said Susan. "Let him have it to play with tomorrow. We'll clear it all away before that nurse comes back with her caps and her collars and her stuck-up cheek."

So next day Philip went on with his building. He put everything you can think of into it: the dominoes and the domino box, bricks and books, cotton reels that he begged from Susan, and a collar box and some cake tins contributed by the cook. He made steps of the dominoes and a terrace of the domino box. He got bits of southern-wood out of the garden and stuck them in cotton reels, which made beautiful pots, and they looked like bay trees in tubs. Brass finger bowls served for domes, and the lids of brass kettles and coffeepots from the oak dresser in the hall made minarets of dazzling splendor. Chessmen were useful for minarets too.

"I must have paved paths and a fountain," said Philip thoughtfully. The paths were paved with mother-of-pearl card counters, and the fountain was a silver and glass ashtray, with a needlecase of filigree silver rising up from the middle of it; and the falling water was made quite nicely out of narrow bits of the silver paper off the chocolate Helen had given him at parting. Palm trees were easily made—Helen had shown him how to do that—with bits of larch fastened to elder stems with plasticine. There was plenty of plasticine among Lucy's toys; there was plenty of everything.

And the city grew, till it covered the table. Philip, unwearied, set about to make another city on another table. This had for chief feature a great water tower, with a fountain around its base; and now he stopped at nothing. He unhooked the crystal drops from the great chandeliers to make his fountains. This city was grander than the first. It had a grand tower made of a wastepaper basket and an astrologer's tower that was a photograph-enlarging machine.

The cities were really very beautiful. I wish I could describe them thoroughly to you. But it would take pages and pages. Besides all the things I have told of alone there were towers and turrets and grand staircases, pagodas and pavilions, canals made bright and waterlike by strips of silver paper, and a lake with a boat on it. Philip put into his buildings all the things out of the dollhouse that seemed suitable. The wooden things-to-eat and dishes. The leaden teacups and goblets. He peopled the place with dominoes and pawns. The handsome chessmen were used for minarets. He made forts and garrisoned them with lead soldiers.

He worked hard and he worked cleverly, and as the cities grew in beauty and interestingness he loved them more and more. He was happy now. There was no time to be unhappy in.

"I will keep it as it is till Helen comes. How she will *love* it!" he said.

The two cities were connected by a bridge which was a yardstick he had found in the servants' sewing room and taken without hindrance, for by this time all the servants were his friends. Susan had been the first—that was all.

He had just laid his bridge in place, and put Mr. and Mrs. Noah in the chief square to represent the inhabitants, and was standing rapt in admiration of his work, when a hard hand on each of his shoulders made him start and scream.

It was the nurse. She had come back a day sooner than anyone expected her. The brother had brought home a wife, and she and the nurse had not liked each other; so she was very cross, and she took

Philip by the shoulders and shook him, a thing which had never happened to him before.

"You naughty, wicked boy!" she said, still shaking.

"But I haven't hurt anything—I'll put everything back," he said, trembling and very pale.

"You'll not touch any of it again," said the nurse. "I'll see to that. I shall put everything away myself in the morning. Taking what doesn't belong to you!"

"But you said I might take anything I liked," said Philip, "so if it's wrong it's your fault."

"You untruthful child!" cried the nurse, and hit him over the knuckles. Now, no one had ever hit Philip before. He grew paler than ever, but he did not cry, though his hands hurt rather badly. For she had snatched up the yardstick to hit him with, and it was hard and cornery.

"You are a coward," said Philip, "and it is you who are untruthful and not me."

"Hold your tongue," said the nurse, and whirled him off to bed.

"You'll get no supper, so there!" she said, angrily tucking him up.

"I don't want any," said Philip, "and I have to forgive you before the sun goes down."

"Forgive, indeed!" said she, flouncing out.

"When you get sorry you'll know I've forgiven you," Philip called after her, which, of course, made her angrier than ever.

Whether Philip cried when he was alone is not our business. Susan, who had watched the shaking and the hitting without daring to interfere, crept up later with milk and sponge cakes. She found him asleep, and she says his eyelashes were wet.

When he awoke he thought at first that it was morning, the room was so light. But presently he saw that it was not yellow sunlight but white moonshine which made the beautiful brightness.

He wondered at first why he felt so unhappy, then he remembered how Helen had gone away and how hateful the nurse had been. And now she would pull down the city and Helen would never see it. And he would never be able to build such a beautiful one again. In the morning it would be gone, and he would not be able even to remember how it was built.

The moonlight was very bright.

"I wonder how my city looks by moonlight," he said.

And then, all in a thrilling instant, he made up his mind to go down and see for himself how it did look.

He slipped on his dressing gown, opened his door softly, and crept along the corridor and down the broad staircase, then along the gallery and into the drawing room. It was very dark, but he felt his way to a window and undid the shutter, and there lay his city, flooded with moonlight, just as he had imagined it.

He gazed on it for a moment in ecstasy and then turned to shut the door. As he did so he felt a slight strange giddiness and stood a moment with his hand to his head. He turned and went again toward the city, and when he was close to it he gave a little cry, hastily stifled, for fear someone should hear him and come down and send him to bed. He stood and gazed about him bewildered and, once more, rather giddy. For the city had, in a quick blink of light, followed by darkness, disappeared. So had the drawing room. So had the chair that stood close to the table. He could see mountainous shapes raising enormous heights in the distance, and the moonlight shone on the tops of them. But he himself seemed to be in a vast, flat plain. There was the softness of long grass around his feet, but there were no trees, no houses, no hedges or fences to break the expanse of grass. It seemed darker in some parts than others. That was all. It reminded him of the illimitable prairie of which he had read in books of adventure.

"I suppose I'm dreaming," said Philip, "though I don't see how I can have gone to sleep just while I was turning the door handle. However—"

He stood still, expecting that something would happen. In dreams something always does happen, if it's only that the dream comes to an end. But nothing happened now—Philip just stood there quite quietly and felt the warm soft grass around his ankles.

Then, as his eyes became used to the darkness of the plain, he saw some way off a very steep bridge leading up to a dark height on whose summit the moon shone whitely. He walked toward it, and as he approached he saw that it was less like a bridge than a sort of ladder, and that it rose to a giddy height above him. It seemed to rest on a rock far up against dark sky, and the inside of the rock seemed hollowed out in one vast dark cave.

And now he was close to the foot of the ladder. It had no rungs, but narrow ledges made hold for feet and hands. Philip remembered Jack and the Beanstalk, and looked up longingly; but the ladder was a very, very long one. On the other hand, it was the only thing that seemed to lead anywhere, and he had had enough of standing lonely in the grassy prairie, where he seemed to have been for a very long time indeed. So he put his hands and feet to the ladder and began to go up. It was a very long climb. There were three hundred and eight steps, for he counted them. And the steps were only on one side of the ladder, so he had to be extremely careful. On he went, up and on, on and up, till his feet ached and his hands felt as though they would drop off for tiredness. He could not look up far, and he dared not look down at all. There was nothing for it but to climb and climb and climb, and at last he saw the ground on which the ladder rested—a terrace hewn in regular lines, and, as it seemed, hewn from the solid rock. His head was level with the ground, now his hands, now his feet. He leaped sideways from the ladder and threw himself facedown on the ground, which was cold and smooth like marble. There he lay, drawing deep breaths of weariness and relief.

There was a great silence all about, which rested and soothed, and presently he rose and looked around him. He was close to an archway with very thick pillars, and he went toward it and peeped cautiously in. It seemed to be a great gate leading to an open space, and beyond it he could see dim piles that looked like churches and houses. But all

*Beyond it he could see dim piles that looked like churches and houses.*

was deserted; the moonlight and he had the place, whatever it was, to themselves.

"I suppose everyone's in bed," said Philip, and stood there trembling a little, but very curious and interested, in the black shadow of the strange arch.

CHAPTER TWO

# Deliverer or Destroyer

PHILIP STOOD in the shadow of the dark arch and looked out. He saw before him a great square surrounded by tall irregular buildings. In the middle was a fountain whose waters, silver in the moonlight, rose and fell with gentle splashing sound. A tall tree, close to the archway, cast the shadow of its trunk across the path—a broad black bar. He listened, listened, listened, but there was nothing to listen to, except the deep night silence and the changing soft sound the fountain made.

His eyes, growing accustomed to the dimness, showed him that he was under a heavy domed roof supported on large square pillars—to the right and left stood dark doors, shut fast.

"I will explore these doors by daylight," he said. He did not feel exactly frightened. But he did not feel exactly brave either. But he wished and intended to be brave, so he said, "I will explore these doors. At least I think I will," he added, for one must not only be brave but truthful.

And then suddenly he felt very sleepy. He leaned against the wall, and presently it seemed that sitting down would be less trouble, and then that lying down would be more truly comfortable. A bell from

19

very, very far away sounded the hour, twelve. Philip counted up to nine, but he missed the tenth bell-beat, and the eleventh and the twelfth as well, because he was fast asleep, cuddled up warmly in the thick quilted dressing gown that Helen had made him last winter. He dreamed that everything was as it used to be before That Man came and changed everything and took Helen away. He was in his own little bed in his own little room in their own little house, and Helen had come to call him. He could see the sunlight through his closed eyelids—he was keeping them closed just for the fun of hearing her try to wake him, and presently he would tell her he had been awake all the time, and they would laugh together about it. And then he awoke, and he was not in his soft bed at home but on the hard floor of a big, strange gatehouse, and it was not Helen who was shaking him and saying, "Here—I say, wake up, can't you?" but a tall man in a red coat; and the light that dazzled his eyes was not from the sun at all, but from a horn lantern that the man was holding close to his face.

"What's the matter?" said Philip sleepily.

"That's the question," said the man in red. "Come along to the guardroom and give an account of yourself, you young shaver."

He took Philip's ear gently but firmly between a very hard finger and thumb.

"Leave go," said Philip, "I'm not going to run away." And he stood up feeling very brave.

The man shifted his hold from ear to shoulder and led Philip through one of those doors which he had thought of exploring by daylight. It was not daylight yet, and the room, large and bare, with an arch at each end and narrow little windows at the sides, was lighted by horn lanterns and tall tapers in pewter candlesticks. It seemed to Philip that the room was full of soldiers.

Their captain, with a good deal of gold about him and a very smart black mustache, got up from a bench.

"Look what I've caught, sir," said the man who owned the hand on Philip's shoulder.

*"Here—I say, wake up, can't you?"*

"Humph," said the captain, "so it's really happened at last."

"What has?" said Philip.

"Why, you have," said the captain. "Don't be frightened, little man."

"I'm not frightened," said Philip, and added politely, "I should be so much obliged if you'd tell me what you mean." He added something that he had heard people say when they asked the way to the market or the public gardens; "I'm quite a stranger here," he said.

A jolly roar of laughter went up from the red-coats.

"It isn't manners to laugh at strangers," said Philip.

"Mind your own manners," said the captain sharply. "In this country little boys speak when they're spoken to. Stranger, eh? Well, we knew that, you know!"

Philip, though he felt snubbed, yet felt grand too. Here he was in the middle of an adventure with grown-up soldiers. He threw out his chest and tried to look manly.

The captain sat down in a chair at the end of a long table, drew a black book to him—a black book covered with dust—and began to rub a rusty pen nib on his sword, which was not rusty.

"Come now," he said, opening the book, "tell me how you came here. And mind you speak the truth."

"I *always* speak the truth," said Philip proudly.

All the soldiers rose and saluted him with looks of deep surprise and respect.

"Well, nearly always," said Philip, hot to the ears, and the soldiers clattered stiffly down again onto the benches, laughing once more. Philip had imagined there to be more discipline in the army.

"How did you come here?" said the captain.

"Up the great bridge staircase," said Philip.

The captain wrote busily in the book.

"What did you come for?"

"I didn't know what else to do. There was nothing but illimitable prairie—and so I came up."

"You are a very bold boy," said the captain.

"Thank you," said Philip. "I do *want* to be."

"What was your purpose in coming?"

"I didn't do it on purpose—I just happened to come."

The captain wrote that down too. And then he and Philip and the soldiers looked at each other in silence.

"Well?" said the boy.

"Well?" said the captain.

"I do wish," said the boy, "you'd tell me what you meant by my really happening after all. And then I wish you'd tell me the way home."

"Where do you want to get to?" asked the captain.

"The *address*," said Philip, "is The Grange, Ravelsham, Sussex."

"Don't know it," said the captain briefly, "and anyhow you can't go back there now. Didn't you read the notice at the top of the ladder? Trespassers will be prosecuted. You've got to be prosecuted before you can go back anywhere."

"I'd rather be persecuted than go down that ladder again," he said. "I suppose it won't be very bad—being persecuted, I mean?"

His idea of persecution was derived from books. He thought it to be something vaguely unpleasant from which one escaped in disguise—adventurous and always successful.

"That's for the judges to decide," said the captain, "it's a serious thing, trespassing in our city. This guard is put here expressly to prevent it."

"Do you have many trespassers?" Philip asked. The captain seemed kind, and Philip had a great-uncle who was a judge, so the word "judges" made him think of tips and good advice, rather than of justice and punishment.

"Many trespassers indeed!" The captain almost snorted his answer. "That's just it. There's never been one before. You're the first. For years and years and years there's been a guard here, because when the town was first built the astrologers foretold that some day there would be a trespasser who would do untold mischief. So it's our privilege—we're the Polistopolitan guards—to keep watch over the only way by which a trespasser could come in."

"May I sit down?" said Philip suddenly, and the soldiers made room for him on the bench.

"My father and my grandfather and all my ancestors were in the guards," said the captain proudly. "It's a very great honor."

"I wonder," said Philip, "why you don't cut off the end of your ladder—the top end I mean; then nobody could come up."

"That would never do," said the captain, "because, you see, there's another prophecy. The great deliverer is to come that way."

"Couldn't I," suggested Philip shyly, "couldn't I be the deliverer instead of the trespasser? I'd much rather, you know."

"I daresay you would," said the captain, "but people can't be deliverers just because they'd much rather, you know."

"And isn't anyone to come up the ladder bridge except just those two?"

"We don't know; that's just it. You know what prophecies are."

"I'm afraid I don't—exactly."

"So vague and mixed up, I mean. The one I'm telling you about goes something like this.

> "Who comes up the ladder stair?
>     Beware, beware,
>   Steely eyes and copper hair
>   Strife and grief and pain to bear
>   All come up the ladder stair.

"You see we can't tell whether that means one person or a lot of people with steely eyes and copper hair."

"My hair's just plain boy-color," said Philip, "my sister says so, and my eyes are blue, I believe."

"I can't see in this light." The captain leaned his elbows on the table and looked earnestly in the boy's eyes. "No, I can't see. The other prophecy goes:

> "From down and down and very far down
> The king shall come to take his own;
> He shall deliver the Magic town,
> And all that he made shall be his own.
> Beware, take care. Beware, prepare,
> The king shall come by the ladder stair."

"How jolly," said Philip. "I love poetry. Do you know any more?"

"There are heaps of prophecies, of course," said the captain. "The astrologers must do something to earn their pay. There's rather a nice one:

> "Every night when the bright stars blink
> The guards shall turn out, and have a drink
> As the clock strikes two.
> And every night when no stars are seen
> The guards shall drink in their own canteen
> When the clock strikes two.

"Tonight there aren't any stars, so we have the drinks served here. It's less trouble than going across the square to the canteen, and the principle's the same. Principle is the great thing with a prophecy, my boy."

"Yes," said Philip. And then the faraway bell beat again. One, two. And outside was a light patter of feet.

A soldier rose—saluted his officer and threw open the door. There was a moment's pause; Philip expected someone to come in with a tray and glasses, as they did at his great-uncle's when gentlemen were suddenly thirsty at times that were not mealtimes.

But instead, after a moment's pause, a dozen greyhounds stepped daintily in on their padded catlike feet; and around the neck of each dog was slung a roundish thing that looked like one of the little barrels that St. Bernard dogs wear around their necks in the pictures. And when these were loosened and laid on the table Philip was charmed to see that the roundish things were not barrels but coconuts.

The soldiers reached down some pewter pots from a high shelf—pierced the coconuts with their bayonets and poured out the coconut milk. They all had drinks, so the prophecy came true, and what is more they gave Philip a drink as well. It was delicious, and there was as much of it as he wanted. I have never had as much coconut milk as I wanted. Have you?

Then the hollow coconuts were tied on to the dogs' necks again and out they went, slim and beautiful, two by two, wagging their slender tails, in the most amiable and orderly way.

"They take the coconuts to the town kitchen," said the captain, "to be made into coconut ice for the army breakfast; waste not want not, you know. We don't waste anything here, my boy." Philip had quite got over his snubbing. He now felt that the captain was talking with him as man to man. Helen had gone away and left him; well, he was learning to do without Helen. And he had got away from the Grange, and Lucy, and that nurse. He was a man among men. And then, just as he was feeling most manly and important, and quite equal to facing any number of judges, there came a little tap at the door of the guardroom, and a very little voice said:

"Oh, do please let me come in."

Then the door opened slowly.

"Well, come in, whoever you are," said the captain. And the person who came in was—Lucy. Lucy, whom Philip thought he had got rid of—Lucy, who stood for the new hateful life to which Helen had left him. Lucy, in her serge skirt and jersey, with her little sleek fair pigtails, and that anxious "I-wish-we-could-be-friends" smile of hers. Philip was furious. It was too bad.

"And who is this?" the captain was saying kindly.

"It's me—it's Lucy," she said. "I came up with *him*."

She pointed to Philip. "No manners," thought Philip in bitterness.

"No, you didn't," he said shortly.

"I did—I was close behind you when you were climbing the ladder bridge. And I've been waiting alone ever since, when you were asleep and all. I *knew* he'd be cross when he knew I'd come," she explained to the soldiers.

"I'm *not* cross," said Philip very crossly indeed, but the captain signed to him to be silent. Then Lucy was questioned and her answers written in the book, and when that was done the captain said:

"So this little girl is a friend of yours?"

"No, she isn't," said Philip violently. "She's not my friend, and she never will be. I've seen her, that's all, and I don't want to see her again."

"You *are* unkind," said Lucy.

And then there was a grave silence, most unpleasant to Philip. The soldiers, he perceived, now looked coldly at him. It was all Lucy's fault. What did she want to come shoving in for, spoiling everything? Anyone but a girl would have known that a guardroom wasn't the right place for a girl. He frowned and said nothing. Lucy had snuggled up against the captain's knee, and he was stroking her hair.

"Poor little woman," he said. "You must go to sleep now, so as to be rested before you go to the Hall of Justice in the morning."

They made Lucy a bed of soldiers' cloaks laid on a bench; and bearskins are the best of pillows. Philip had a soldier's cloak and a bench, and a bearskin too—but what was the good? Everything was spoiled. If Lucy had not come the guardroom as a sleeping place would have been almost as good as the tented field. But she *had* come, and the guardroom was no better now than any old night nursery. And how had she known? How had she come? How had she made her way to that illimitable prairie where he had found the mysterious beginning of the ladder bridge? He went to sleep a bunched-up lump of prickly discontent and suppressed fury.

When he woke it was bright daylight, and a soldier was saying, "Wake up, Trespassers. Breakfast—"

"How jolly," thought Philip, "to be having military breakfast." Then he remembered Lucy, and hated her being there, and felt once more that she had spoiled everything.

I should not, myself, care for a breakfast of coconut ice, peppermint creams, apples, bread and butter and sweet milk. But the soldiers seemed to enjoy it. And it would have exactly suited Philip if he had not seen that Lucy was enjoying it too.

"I do hate greedy girls," he told himself, for he was now in that state of black rage when you hate everything the person you are angry with does or says or is.

And now it was time to start for the Hall of Justice. The guard formed outside, and Philip noticed that each soldier stood on a sort of green mat. When the order to march was given, each soldier quickly and expertly rolled up his green mat and put it under his arm. And whenever they stopped, because of the crowd, each soldier unrolled his green mat, and stood on it till it was time to go on again. And they had to stop several times, for the crowd was very thick in the great squares and in the narrow streets of the city. It was a wonderful crowd. There were men and women and children in every sort of dress. Italian, Spanish, Russian; French peasants in blue blouses and wooden shoes, workmen in the dress English working people wore a hundred years ago. Norwegians, Swedes, Swiss, Turks, Greeks, Indians, Arabians, Chinese, Japanese, besides Red Indians in dresses of skins, and Scots in kilts and sporrans. Philip did not know what nation most of the dresses belonged to—to him it was a brilliant patchwork of gold and gay colors. It reminded him of the fancy-dress party he had once been to with Helen, when he wore a Pierrot's dress and felt very silly in it. He noticed that not a single boy in all that crowd was dressed as he was—in what he thought was the only correct dress for boys. Lucy walked beside him. Once, just after they started, she said, "Aren't you frightened, Philip?" and he would not answer, though he longed to say, "Of course not. It's only girls who are afraid." But he thought it would be more disagreeable to say nothing, so he said it.

When they got to the Hall of Justice, she caught hold of his hand, and said:

"Oh!" very loud and sudden. "Doesn't it remind you of anything?" she asked.

Philip pulled his hand away and said "No" before he remembered that he had decided not to speak to her. And the "No" was quite untrue, for the building did remind him of something, though he couldn't have told you what.

The prisoners and their guard passed through a great arch between magnificent silver pillars, and along a vast corridor, lined with soldiers who all saluted.

"Do all sorts of soldiers salute you?" he asked the captain, "or only just your own ones?"

"It's *you* they're saluting," the captain said. "Our laws tell us to salute all prisoners out of respect for their misfortunes."

The judge sat on a high bronze throne with colossal bronze dragons on each side of it, and wide shallow steps of ivory, black, and white.

Two attendants spread a round mat on the top of the steps in front of the judge—a yellow mat it was, and very thick, and he stood up and saluted the prisoners. ("Because of your misfortunes," the captain whispered.)

The judge wore a bright yellow robe with a green girdle, and he had no wig, but a very odd-shaped hat, which he kept on all the time.

The trial did not last long, and the captain said very little, and the judge still less, while the prisoners were not allowed to speak at all. The judge looked up something in a book, and consulted in a low voice with the crown lawyer and a sour-faced person in black. Then he put on his spectacles and said:

"Prisoners at the bar, you are found guilty of trespass. The punishment is Death—if the judge does not like the prisoners. If he does not dislike them it is imprisonment for life, or until the judge has had time to think it over. Remove the prisoners."

"Oh, *don't!*" cried Philip, almost weeping.

"I thought you weren't afraid," whispered Lucy.

"Silence in court," said the judge.

Then Philip and Lucy were removed.

They were marched by streets quite different from those they had come by, and at last in the corner of a square they came to a large house that was quite black.

"Here we are," said the captain kindly. "Good-bye. Better luck next time."

The jailer, a gentleman in black velvet, with a ruff and a pointed beard, came out and welcomed them cordially.

"How do you do, my dears?" he said. "I hope you'll be comfortable here. First-class misdemeanants, I suppose?" he asked.

"Of course," said the captain.

"Top floor, if you please," said the jailer politely, and stood back to let the children pass. "Turn to the left and up the stairs."

The stairs were dark and went on and on, and around and around, and up and up. At the very top was a big room, simply furnished with a table, chairs, and a rocking horse. Who wants more furniture than that?

"You've got the best view in the whole city," said the jailer, "and you'll be company for me. What? They gave me the post of jailer because it's nice, light, gentlemanly work, and leaves me time for my writing. I'm a literary man, you know. But I've sometimes found it a trifle lonely. You're the first prisoners I've ever had, you see. If you'll excuse me I'll go and order some dinner for you. You'll be contented with the feast of reason and the flow of soul, I feel certain."

The moment the door had closed on the jailer's black back Philip turned on Lucy.

"I hope you're satisfied," he said bitterly. "This is all *your* doing. They'd have let me off if you hadn't been here. What on earth did you

*"Top floor, if you please," said the jailer politely.*

want to come here for? Why did you come running after me like that? You know I don't like you."

"You're the hatefullest, disagreeablest, horridest boy in all the world," said Lucy firmly. "There!"

Philip had not expected this. He met it as well as he could.

"I'm not a little sneak of a white mouse squeezing in where I'm not wanted, anyhow," he said.

And then they stood looking at each other, breathing quickly, both of them.

"I'd rather be a white mouse than a cruel bully," said Lucy at last.

"I'm not a bully," said Philip.

Then there was another silence. Lucy sniffed. Philip looked around the bare room, and suddenly it came to him that he and Lucy were companions in misfortune, no matter whose fault it was that they were imprisoned. So he said:

"Look here, I don't like you and I shan't pretend I do. But I'll call it Pax for the present if you like. We've got to escape from this place somehow, and I'll help you if you like, and you may help me if you can."

"Thank you," said Lucy, in a tone which might have meant anything.

"So we'll call it Pax and see if we can escape by the window. There might be ivy—or a faithful page with a rope ladder. Have you a page at the Grange?"

"There's two stable boys," said Lucy, "but I don't think they're faithful, and I say, I think all this is much more magic than you think."

"Of course I know it's magic," said he impatiently, "but it's quite real too."

"Oh, it's real enough," said she.

They leaned out of the window. Alas, there was no ivy. Their window was very high up, and the wall outside, when they touched it with their hands, felt smooth as glass.

"*That's* no go," said he, and the two leaned still farther out of the window, looking down on the town. There were strong towers and fine minarets and palaces, the palm trees and fountains and gardens. A white building across the square looked strangely familiar. Could it be like St. Paul's, which Philip had been taken to see when he was very little, and which he had never been able to remember? No, he could not remember it even now. The two prisoners looked out in a long silence. Far below lay the city, its trees softly waving in the breeze, flowers shining in a bright many-colored patchwork, the canals that intersected the big squares gleamed in the sunlight, and crossing and recrossing the squares and streets were the people of the town, coming and going about their business.

"Look here!" said Lucy suddenly. "Do you mean to say you don't know?"

"Know what?" he asked impatiently.

"Where we are. What it is. Don't you?"

"No. No more do you."

"Haven't you seen it all before?"

"No, of course I haven't. No more have you.

"All right. I *have* seen it before, though," said Lucy, "and so have you. But I shan't tell you what it is unless you'll be nice to me." Her tone was a little sad, but quite firm.

"I *am* nice to you. I told you it was Pax," said Philip. "Tell me what you think it is."

"I don't mean that sort of grandish standoffish Pax, but real Pax. Oh, don't be so horrid, Philip. I'm dying to tell you—but I won't if you go on being like you are."

"*I'm* all right," said Philip. "Out with it."

"No. You've got to say it's Pax, and I will stand by you till we get out of this, and I'll always act like a noble friend to you, and I'll try my best to like you. Of course if you can't like me you can't, but you ought to try. Say it after me, won't you?"

Her tone was so kind and persuading that he found himself saying after her, "I, Philip, agree to try and like you, Lucy, and to stand by you till we're out of this, and always to act the part of a noble friend to you. And it's real Pax. Shake hands."

"Now then," said he when they had shaken hands, and Lucy uttered these words:

"Don't you see? It's your own city that we're in, your own city that you built on the tables in the drawing room! It's all got big by magic, so that we could get in. Look"—she pointed out of the window—"see that great golden dome, that's one of the brass fingerbowls, and that white building's my old model of St. Paul's. And there's Buckingham Palace over there, with the carved squirrel on the top, and the chessmen, and the blue-and-white china pepper pots; and the building we're in is the black Japanese cabinet."

Philip looked and he saw that what she said was true. It *was* his city.

"But I didn't build insides to my buildings," said he, "and when did *you* see what I built, anyway?"

"The insides are part of the magic, I suppose," Lucy said, "and I saw the cities you built when Auntie brought me home last night, after you'd been sent to bed. And I did love them. And oh, Philip, I'm so glad it's Pax because I do think you're so *frightfully* clever, and Auntie thought so too, building those beautiful things. And I knew nurse was going to pull it all down. I begged her not to, but she was adamant, and so I got up and dressed and came down to have another look by moonlight. And one or two of the bricks and chessmen had fallen down. I expect nurse knocked them down. So I built them up again as well as I could—and I was loving it all like anything; and then the door opened and I hid under the table, and you came in."

"Then you were there—did you notice how the magic began?"

"No, but it all changed to grass; and then I saw you a long way off going up a ladder. And so I went after you. But I didn't let you see me. I knew you'd be so cross. And then I looked in at the guardroom door, and I did so want some of the coconut milk."

"When did you find out it was *my* city?"

"I thought the soldiers looked like my lead ones somehow. But I wasn't sure till I saw the judge. Why he's just old Noah, out of the Ark."

"So he is," cried Philip. "How wonderful! How perfectly wonderful! I wish we weren't prisoners. Wouldn't it be jolly to go all over it—into all the buildings, to see what the insides of them have turned into? And all the other people. I didn't put *them* in."

"That's more magic, I expect. But—oh, we shall find it all out in time."

She clapped her hands. And on the instant the door opened and the jailer appeared.

"A visitor for you," he said, and stood aside to let someone else come in, someone tall and thin, with a black hooded cloak and a black half-mask, such as people wear at carnival time.

When the jailer had shut the door and gone away the tall figure took off its mask and let fall its cloak, showing to the surprised but recognizing eyes of the children the well-known shape of Mr. Noah—the judge.

"How do you do?" he said. "This is a little unofficial visit. I hope I haven't come at an inconvenient time."

"We're very glad," said Lucy, "because you can tell us."

"I won't answer questions," said Mr. Noah, sitting down stiffly on his yellow mat, "but I will tell you something. We don't know who you are. But I myself think that you may be the Deliverer."

"Both of us," said Philip jealously.

"One or both. You see, the prophecy says that the Destroyer's hair is red. And your hair is not red. But before I could get the populace to feel sure of that, my own hair would be gray with thought and argument. Some people are so wooden-headed. And I am not used to thinking. I don't often have to do it. It distresses me."

The children said they were sorry. Philip added:

"Do tell us a little about your city. It isn't a question. We want to know if it's magic. That isn't a question either."

"I was about to tell you," said Mr. Noah, "and I will not answer questions. Of course it is magic. Everything in the world is magic, until you understand it.

"And as to the city. I will just tell you a little of our history. Many thousand years ago all the cities of our country were built by a great and powerful giant, who brought the materials from far and wide. The place was peopled partly by persons of his choice, and partly by a sort of self-acting magic rather difficult to explain. As soon as the cities were built and the inhabitants placed here the life of the city began, and it was, to those who lived it, as though it had always been. The artisans toiled, the musicians played, and the poets sang. The astrologers, finding themselves in a tall tower evidently designed for such a purpose, began to observe the stars and to prophesy."

"I know that part," said Philip.

"Very well," said the judge. "Then you know quite enough. Now I want to ask a little favor of you both. Would you mind escaping?"

"If we only could," Lucy sighed.

"The strain on my nerves is too much," said Mr. Noah feelingly. "Escape, my dear children, to please me, a very old man in indifferent health and poor spirits."

"But how—"

"Oh, you just walk out. You, my boy, can disguise yourself in your dressing gown, which I see has been placed on yonder chair, and I will leave my cloak for you, little girl."

They both said "Thank you," and Lucy added: "But *how?*"

"Through the door," said the judge. "There is a rule about putting prisoners on their honor not to escape, but there have not been any prisoners for so long that I don't suppose they put you on honor. No? You can just walk out of the door. There are many charitable persons in the city who will help to conceal you. The front-door key turns easily, and I myself will oil it as I go out. Good-bye—thank you so much for falling in with my little idea. Accept an old man's blessing. Only don't tell the jailer. He would never forgive me."

He got off his mat, rolled it up and went.

"Well!" said Lucy.

"Well!" said Philip.

"I suppose we go?" he said. But Lucy said, "What about the jailer? Won't he catch it if we bolt?"

Philip felt this might be true. It was annoying, and as bad as being put on one's honor.

"Bother!" was what he said.

And then the jailer came in. He looked pale and worried.

"I am so awfully sorry," he began. "I thought I should enjoy having you here, but my nerves are all anyhow. The very sound of your voices. I can't write a line. My brain reels. I wonder whether you'd be good enough to do a little thing for me? Would you mind escaping?"

"But won't you get into trouble?"

"Nothing could be worse than this," said the jailer, with feeling. "I had no idea that children's voices were so penetrating. Go, go. I implore you to escape. Only don't tell the judge. I am sure he would never forgive me."

After that, what prisoner would not immediately have escaped?

The two children only waited till the sound of the jailer's keys had died away on the stairs to open their door, run down the many steps, and slip out of the prison gate. They walked a little way in silence. There were plenty of people about, but no one seemed to notice them.

"Which way shall we go?" Lucy asked. "I wish we'd asked him where the Charitables live."

"I think," Philip began, but Lucy was not destined to know what he thought.

There was a sudden shout, a clattering of horses' hooves, and all the faces in the square turned their way.

"They've seen us," cried Philip. "Run, run, run!"

He himself ran, and he ran toward the gatehouse that stood at the top of the ladder stairs by which they had come up, and behind him came the shouting and clatter of hot pursuit. The captain stood in the gateway alone, and just as Philip reached the gate the captain turned into the guardroom and pretended not to see anything. Philip had never run so far or so fast. His breath came in deep sobs, but he reached the ladder and began quickly to go down. It was easier than going up.

He was nearly at the bottom when the whole ladder bridge leaped wildly into the air, and he fell from it and rolled in the thick grass of that illimitable prairie.

All about him the air was filled with great sounds, like the noise of the earthquakes that destroy beautiful big places, and factories that are big but not beautiful. It was deafening, it was endless, it was unbearable.

Yet he had to bear that, and more. And now he felt a curious swelling sensation in his hands, then in his head—then all over. It was extremely painful. He rolled over in his agony, and saw the foot of an enormous giant quite close to him. The foot had a large, flat, ugly shoe, and seemed to come out of gray, low-hanging, swaying curtains. There was a gigantic column too, black against the gray. The ladder bridge, cast down, lay on the ground not far from him.

Pain and fear overcame Philip, and he ceased to hear or feel or know anything.

When he recovered consciousness he found himself under the table in the drawing room. The swelling feeling was over, and he did not seem to be more than his proper size.

He could see the flat feet of the nurse and the lower part of her gray skirt, and a rattling and rumbling on the table above told him that she was doing as she had said she would, and destroying his city. He saw also a black column, which was the leg of the table. Every now and then the nurse walked away to put back into its proper place something he had used in the building. And once she stood on a chair, and he heard the tinkling of the lustre-drops as she hooked them into their places on the chandelier.

"If I lie very still," said he, "perhaps she won't see me. But I

*And behind him . . . the clatter of hot pursuit.*

do wonder how I got here. And what a dream to tell Helen about!"

He lay very still. The nurse did not see him. And when she had gone to her breakfast Philip crawled out.

Yes, the city was gone. Not a trace of it. The very tables were back in their proper places.

Philip went back to his proper place, which, of course, was bed.

"What a splendid dream," he said, as he cuddled down between the sheets, "and now it's all over!"

Of course, he was quite wrong.

# CHAPTER THREE

PHILIP WENT to sleep, and dreamed that he was at home again and that Helen had come to his bedside to call him, leading a white pony that was to be his very own. It was a pony that looked clever enough for anything, and he was not surprised when it shook hands with him; but when it said, "Well, we must be moving," and began to try to put on Philip's shoes and stockings, Philip called out, "Here, I say, stop that," and awoke to a room full of sunshine, but empty of ponies.

"Oh, well," said Philip, "I suppose I'd better get up." He looked at his new silver watch, one of Helen's parting presents, and saw that it marked ten o'clock.

"I say, you know," said he to the watch, "you can't be right." And he shook it to encourage it to think over the matter. But the watch still said "ten" quite plainly and unmistakably.

Now the Grange breakfast time was at eight. And Philip was certain he had not been called.

"This is jolly rum," he remarked. "It must be the watch. Perhaps it's stopped."

But it hadn't stopped. Therefore it must be two hours past breakfast time. The moment he had thought this he became extremely hungry. He got out of bed as soon as he knew exactly how hungry he was.

There was no one about, so he made his way to the bathroom and spent a happy hour with the hot water and the cold water, and the brown Windsor soap and the shaving soap and the nail brush and the flesh brush and the loofahs and the shower bath and the three sponges. He had not, so far, been able thoroughly to investigate and enjoy all these things. But now there was no one to interfere, and he enjoyed himself to that degree that he quite forgot to wonder why he hadn't been called. He thought of a piece of poetry that Helen had made for him, about the bath; and when he had done playing he lay on his back in water that was very hot indeed, trying to remember the poetry. The water was very nearly cold by the time he had remembered the poetry. It was called "Dreams of a Giant Life," and this was it.

### DREAMS OF A GIANT LIFE

What was I once—in ages long ago?
I look back, and I see myself. We grow
So changed through changing years, I hardly see
How that which I look back on could be me?[1]

Glorious and splendid, giant-like I stood
On a white cliff, topped by a darkling wood.
Below me, placid, bright and sparkling, lay
The equal waters of a lovely bay.
White cliffs surrounded it—and calm and fair
It lay asleep, in warm and silent air.

I stood alone—naked and strong, upright
My limbs gleamed in the clear pure golden light.
I saw below me all the water lie
Expecting something, and that thing was I.[2]

---

[1] Never mind grammar.
[2] This is correct grammar, but never mind.

# Lost

I leaned, I plunged, the waves splashed over me.
I lay, a giant in a little sea.

White cliffs all round, wood-crowned, and as I lay
I saw the glories of the dying day;
No wind disturbed my sea; the sunlight was
As though it came through windows of gold glass.
The white cliffs rose above me, and around
The clear sea lay, pure, perfect, and profound;
And I was master of the cliffs, the sea,
And the gold light that brightened over me.

Far miles away my giant feet showed plain,
Rising, like rocks out of the quiet main.
On them a lighthouse could be built, to show
Wayfaring ships the way they must not go.

I was the master of that cliff-girt sea.
I splashed my hands, the waves went over me,
And in the dimples of my body lay
Little rock pools, where small sea beasts might play.

I found a boat, its deck was perforate;
I launched it, and it dared the storms of fate.
Its woolen sail stood out against the sky,
Supported by a mast of ivory.

Another boat rode proudly to my hand,
Upon its deck a thousand spears did stand;
I launched it, and it sped full fierce and fast
Against the boat that had the ivory mast
And woolen sail and perforated deck.
The two went down in one stupendous wreck!

Beneath the waves I chased with joyous hand
Upon the bed of an imagined sand
The slippery brown sea mouse, that still escaped,
Where the deep cave beneath my knee was shaped.
Caught it at last and caged it into rest
Upon the shallows of my submerged breast.

Then, as I lay, wrapped as in some kind arm
By the sweet world of waters soft and warm,
A great voice cried, from some far unseen shore,
And I was not a giant anymore.

"Come out, come out," cried out the voice of power.
"You've been in for a quarter of an hour.
The water's cold—come, Master Pip—your head's
all wet, and it is time you were in bed."

I rose all dripping from the magic sea
And left the ships that had been slaves to me—
The soap dish, with its perforated deck,
The nailbrush, that had rushed to loss and wreck,
The flannel sail, the toothbrush that was mast,
The sleek soap mouse—I left them all at last.

I went out of that magic sea and cried
Because the time came when I must be dried
And leave the splendor of a giant's joy
And go to bed—a little well-washed boy.

When he had quite remembered the poetry he had another
shower bath, and then when he had enjoyed the hot rough towels out
of the hot cupboard he went back to his room to dress. He now felt

how deeply he wanted his breakfast, so he dressed himself with all possible speed, even forgetting to fasten his bootlaces properly. He was in such a hurry that he dropped his collar stud, and it was as he stooped to pick it up that he remembered his dream. Do you know that was really the first time he had thought of it. The dream—that indeed would be something to think about.

Breakfast was the really important thing. He went down very hungry indeed. "I shall ask for my breakfast directly I get down," he said. "I shall ask the first person I meet." And he met no one.

There was no one on the stairs, or in the hall, or in the dining room, or in the drawing room. The library and billiard room were empty of living people, and the door of the nursery was locked. So then Philip made his way into the regions beyond the baize door, where the servants' quarters were. And there was no one in the kitchen, or in the servants' hall, or in the butler's pantry, or in the scullery, or the washhouse, or the larder. In all that big house, and it was much bigger than it looked from the front because of the long wings that ran out on each side of its back—in all that big house there was no one but Philip. He felt certain of this before he ran upstairs and looked in all the bedrooms and in the little picture gallery and the music room, and then in the servants' bedrooms and the very attics. There were interesting things in those attics, but Philip only remembered that afterward. Now he tore down the stairs three at a time. All the room doors were open as he had left them, and somehow those open doors frightened him more than anything else. He ran along the corridors, down more stairs, past more open doors, and out through the back kitchen, along the moss-grown walk by the brick wall and so around by the three yew trees and the mounting block to the stable yard. And there was no one there. Neither coachman nor groom nor stable boys. And there was no one in the stables, or the coach house, or the harness room, or the loft.

Philip felt that he could not go back into the house. Something terrible must have happened. Was it possible that anyone could want the Grange servants enough to kidnap them? Philip thought of the nurse and felt that, at least as far as she was concerned, it was *not* possible. Or perhaps it was magic! A sort of Sleeping Beauty happening! Only everyone had vanished instead of just being put to sleep for a hundred years.

He was alone in the middle of the stable yard when the thought came to him.

"Perhaps they're only made invisible. Perhaps they're all here and watching me and making fun of me."

He stood still to think this. It was not a pleasant thought.

Suddenly he straightened his little back, and threw back his head.

"They shan't see I'm frightened anyway," he told himself. And then he remembered the larder.

"I haven't had any breakfast," he explained aloud, so as to be plainly heard by any invisible people who might be about. "I ought to have my breakfast. If nobody gives it to me I shall take my breakfast."

He waited for an answer. But none came. It was very quiet in the stable yard. Only the rattle of a halter ring against a manger, the sound of a hoof on stable stones, the cooing of pigeons, and the rustle of straw in the loose box broke the silence.

"Very well," said Philip. "I don't know what *you* think I ought to have for breakfast, so I shall take what *I* think."

He drew a long breath, trying to draw courage in with it, threw back his shoulders more soldierly than ever, and marched in through the back door and straight to the larder. Then he took what he thought he ought to have for breakfast. This is what he thought:

> 1 cherry pie,
> 2 custards in cups,
> 1 cold sausage,
> 2 pieces of cold toast,
> 1 piece of cheese,
> 2 lemon cheesecakes,
> 1 small jam tart (there was only one left),
> Butter, 1 pat.

"What jolly things the servants have to eat," he said. "I never knew. I thought that nothing but mutton and rice grew here."

He put all the food on a silver tray and carried it out onto the terrace, which lay between the two wings at the back of the house. Then he went back for milk, but there was none to be seen so he got a white jug full of water. The spoons he couldn't find, but he found a carving fork and a fish slice. Did you ever try to eat cherry pie with a fish slice?

"Whatever's happened," said Philip to himself, through the cherry pie, "and whatever happens it's as well to have had your breakfast." And he bit a generous inch off the cold sausage, which he had speared with the carving fork.

And now, sitting out in the good sunshine, and growing less and less hungry as he plied fish slice and carving fork, his mind went back to his dream, which began to seem more and more real. Suppose it really *had* happened? It might have; magic things did happen, it seemed. Look how all the people had vanished out of the house—out of the world too, perhaps.

"Suppose everyone's vanished," said Philip. "Suppose I'm the only person left in the world who hasn't vanished. Then everything in the world would belong to me. Then I could have everything that's in all the toy shops." And his mind for a moment dwelt fondly on this beautiful idea.

Then he went on. "But suppose I vanished too? Perhaps if I were to vanish I could see the other people who have. I wonder how it's done."

He held his breath and tried hard to vanish. Have you ever tried this? It is not at all easy to do. Philip could not do it at all. He held his breath and he tried and he tried, but he only felt fatter and fatter and more and more as though in one more moment he should burst. So he let his breath go.

"No," he said, looking at his hands. "I'm not any more invisible than I was before. Not so much, I think," he added thoughtfully, looking at what was left of the cherry pie. "But that dream—"

He plunged deep in the remembrance of it that was, to him, like swimming in the waters of a fairy lake.

He was hooked out of his lake suddenly by voices. It was like waking up. There, away across the green park beyond the sunk fence, were people coming.

"So everyone hasn't vanished," he said, caught up the tray, and took it in. He hid it under the pantry shelf. He didn't know who the people were who were coming and you can't be too careful. Then he went out and made himself small in the shadow of a red buttress, heard their voices coming nearer and nearer. They were all talking at once, in that quick, interested way that makes you certain something unusual has happened.

He could not hear exactly what they were saying, but he caught the words:

"No."

"Of course I've asked."

"Police."

"Telegram."

"Yes, of course."

"Better make quite sure."

Then everyone began speaking all at once, and you could not hear anything that anybody said. Philip was too busy keeping behind the buttress to see who they were who were talking. He was glad *something* had happened.

"Now I shall have something to think about besides the nurse and my beautiful city that she has pulled down."

But what was it that had happened? He hoped nobody was hurt—or had done anything wrong. The word "police" had always made him uncomfortable ever since he had seen a boy no bigger than himself pulled along the road by a very large policeman. The boy had stolen a loaf, Philip was told. Philip could never forget that boy's face; he always thought of it in church when it said "prisoners and captives," and still more when it said "desolate and oppressed."

"I do hope it's not *that*," he said.

And slowly he got himself to leave the shelter of the redbrick buttress and to follow to the house those voices and those footsteps that had gone by him.

He followed the sound of them to the kitchen. The cook was there in tears and a Windsor armchair. The kitchen maid, her cap all on one side, was crying down most dirty cheeks. The coachman was there, very red in the face, and the groom, without his gaiters. The nurse was there, neat as ever she seemed at first, but Philip was delighted when a more careful inspection showed him that there was mud on her large shoes and on the bottom of her skirt, and that her dress had a large three-cornered tear in it.

"I wouldn't have had it happen for a twenty-pun note," the coachman was saying.

"George," said the nurse to the groom, "you go and get a horse ready. I'll write the telegram."

"You'd best take Peppermint," said the coachman. "She's the fastest."

The groom went out, saying under his breath, "Teach your grandmother," which Philip thought rude and unmeaning.

Philip was standing unnoticed by the door. He felt that thrill—if it isn't pleasure it is more like it than anything else—which we all feel when something real has happened.

But what *had* happened. What?

"I wish I'd never come back," said the nurse. "Then nobody could pretend it was *my* fault.

"It don't matter what they pretend," the cook stopped crying to say. "The thing is what's happened. Oh, my goodness. I'd rather have been turned away without a character than have had this happen."

"And I'd rather *any*thing," said the nurse. "Oh, my goodness me. I wish I'd never been born."

And then and there, before the astonished eyes of Philip, she began to behave as any nice person might—she began to cry.

49

"It wouldn't have happened," said the cook, "if the master hadn't been away. He's a Justice of the Peace, he is, and a terror to gypsies. It wouldn't never have happened if—"

Philip could not bear it any longer.

"*What* wouldn't have happened if?" he asked, startling everybody to a quick jump of surprise.

The nurse stopped crying and turned to look at him.

"Oh, *you!*" she said slowly. "I forgot *you*. You want your breakfast, I suppose, no matter what's happened?"

"No, I don't," said Philip, with extreme truth. "I want to know what *has* happened?"

"Miss Lucy's lost," said the cook heavily, "that's what's happened. So now you know. You run along and play, like a good little boy, and don't make extry trouble for us in the trouble we're in."

"Lost?" repeated Philip.

"Yes, lost. I expect you're glad," said the nurse, "the way you treated her. You hold your tongue and don't let me so much as hear you breathe the next twenty-four hours. I'll go and write that telegram."

Philip thought it best not to let anyone hear him breathe. By this means he heard the telegram when nurse read it aloud to the cook.

"Peter Graham, Esq.,
Hotel Wagram,
Brussels.
Miss Lucy lost. Please come home immediately.
PHILKINS

That's all right, isn't it?"

"I don't see why you sign it "Philkins". You're only the nurse— I'm the head of the house when the family's away, and my name's Bobson," the cook said.

There was a sound of torn paper.

"There—the paper's tore. I'd just as soon your name went to it," said the nurse. "I don't want to be the one to tell such news."

"Oh, my good gracious, what a thing to happen," sighed the cook. "Poor little darling!"

Then somebody wrote the telegram again, and the nurse took it out to the stable yard, where Peppermint was already saddled.

"I thought," said Philip, bold in the nurse's absence, "I thought Lucy was with her aunt."

"She came back yesterday," said the cook. "Yes, after you'd gone to bed. And this morning that nurse went into the night nursery and she wasn't there. Her bed all empty and cold, and her clothes gone. Though how the gypsies could have got in without waking that nurse is a mystery to me and ever will be. She must sleep like a pig."

"Or the seven sleepers," said the coachman.

"But what would gypsies want her *for*?" Philip asked.

"What do they ever want anybody for?" retorted the cook. "Look at the heirs that's been stolen. I don't suppose there's a titled family in England but what's had its heir stolen, one time and another."

"I suppose you've looked all over the house," said Philip.

"I suppose we ain't deaf and dumb and blind and silly," said the cook. "Here's that nurse. You be off, Mr. Philip, without you want a flea in your ear."

And Philip, at the word, *was* off. He went into the long drawing room, and shut the door. Then he got the ivory chessmen out of the Buhl cabinet, and set them out on that delightful chess table whose checkers are of mother-of-pearl and ivory, and tried to play a game, right hand against left. But right hand, who was white, and so moved first, always won. He gave up after a while, and put the chessmen away in their proper places. Then he got out the big book of photographs of pictures, but they did not seem interesting, so he tried the ivory spillikins. But his hand shook, and you know spillikins is a game you can't play when your hand shakes. And all the time, behind the chess and the pictures and the spillikins, he was trying not to think about his dream, about how he had climbed that ladder stair, which was really the yardstick, and gone into the cities that he had built on the tables. Somehow he did not want to remember it. The very idea of remembering made him feel guilty and wretched.

He went and looked out of the window, and as he stood there his wish not to remember the dream made his boots restless, and in their shuffling his right boot kicked against something hard that lay in the folds of the blue brocade curtain.

He looked down, stooped, and picked up little Mr. Noah. The nurse must have dropped it there when she cleared away the city.

And as he looked upon those wooden features it suddenly became impossible not to think of the dream. He let the remembrance of it come, and it came in a flood. And with it the remembrance of what he had done. He had promised to be Lucy's noble friend, and they had run together to escape from the galloping soldiers. And he had run faster than she. And at the top of the ladder—the ladder of safety—*he had not waited for her.*

"Any old hero would have waited for her, and let her go first," he told himself. "Any gentleman would—even any man—let alone a hero. And I just bunked down the ladder and forgot her. I *left* her there."

Remorse stirred his boots more ungently than before.

"But it was only a dream," he said. And then remorse said, as he had felt all along that it would if he only gave it a chance:

"But suppose it wasn't a dream—suppose it was real. Suppose you *did* leave her there, my noble friend, and that's why she's lost."

Suddenly Philip felt very small, very forlorn, very much alone in the world. But Helen would come back. That telegram would bring her.

Yes. And he would have to tell her that perhaps it was his fault.

It was in vain that Philip told himself that Helen would never believe about the city. He felt that she would. Why shouldn't she? She knew about the fairy tales and the Arabian Nights. And she would know that these things *did* happen.

"Oh, what shall I do? What shall I do?" he said, quite loud. And there was no one but himself to give the answer.

"If I could only get back into the city," he said. "But that hateful nurse has pulled it all down and locked up the nursery. So I can't even build it again. Oh, what *shall* I do?"

And with that he began to cry. For now he felt quite sure that the dream wasn't a dream—that he really *had* gotten into the magic city, had promised to stand by Lucy, and had been false to his promise and to her.

He rubbed his eyes with his knuckles and also—rather painfully—with Mr. Noah, whom he still held. "What shall I do?" he sobbed.

And a very, very teeny tiny voice said:

"Put me down."

"Eh?" said Philip.

"Put me down," said the voice again. It was such a teeny tiny voice that he could only just hear it. It was unlikely, of course, that the voice could have been Mr. Noah's; but then whose else could it be? On the bare chance that it *might* have been Mr. Noah who spoke—more unlikely things had happened before, as you know—Philip set the little wooden figure down on the chess table. It stood there, wooden as ever.

"Put *who* down?" Philip asked. And then, before his eyes, the little wooden figure grew alive, stooped to pick up the yellow disc of wood on which Noah's Ark people stand, rolled it up like a mat, put it under his arm, and began to walk toward the side of the table where Philip stood.

He knelt down to bring his ears nearer the little live moving thing.

"*What* did you say?" he asked, for he fancied that Mr. Noah had again spoken.

"I said, what's the matter?" said the little voice.

"It's Lucy. She's lost and it's my fault. And I can only just hear you. It hurts my ears hearing you," complained Philip.

"There's an ear trumpet in a box on the middle of the cabinet," he could just hear the teeny tiny voice say. "It belonged to a great-aunt. Get it out and listen through it."

53

Philip got it out. It was an odd, curly thing, and at first he could not be sure which end he ought to put to his ear. But he tried both ends, and on the second trial he heard quite a loud, strong, big voice say:

"That's better."

"Then it wasn't a dream last night," said Philip.

"Of course it wasn't," said Mr. Noah.

"Then where is Lucy?"

"In the city, of course. Where you left her."

"But she *can't* be," said Philip desperately. "The city's all pulled down and gone forever."

"The city you built in this room is pulled down," said Mr. Noah, "but the city you went to wasn't in this room. Now, I put it to you—how could it be?"

"But it *was*," said Philip, "or else how could I have gotten into it?"

"It's a little difficult, I own," said Mr. Noah. "But, you see, you built those cities in two worlds. It's pulled down in *this* world. But in the other world it's going on."

"I don't understand," said Philip.

"I thought you wouldn't," said Mr. Noah, "but it's true, for all that. Everything people make in that world goes on forever."

"But how was it that I got in?"

"Because you belong to both worlds. And you built the cities. So they were yours.

"But Lucy got in."

"She built up a corner of your city that the nurse had knocked down."

"But *you*," said Philip, more and more bewildered. "You're here. So you can't be there."

"But I *am* there," said Mr. Noah.

"But you're here. And you're alive here. What made you come alive?"

"Your tears," said Mr. Noah. "Tears are very strong magic. No, don't begin to cry again. What's the matter?"

*He heard quite a loud, strong, big voice say: "That's better."*

"I want to get back into the city."

"It's dangerous."

"I don't care."

"You were glad enough to get away," said Mr. Noah.

"I know: that's the worst of it," said Philip. "Oh, isn't there any way to get back? If I climbed in at the nursery windows and got the bricks and built it all up and—"

"Quite unnecessary, I assure you. There are a thousand doors to that city."

"I wish I could find *one*," said Philip. "But, I say, I thought time was all different there. How is it Lucy is lost all this time if time doesn't count?"

"It does count now," said Mr. Noah. "You made it count when you ran away and left Lucy. That set the clocks of the city to the time of this world."

"I don't understand," said Philip, "but it doesn't matter. Show me the door and I'll go back and find Lucy."

"Build something and go through it," said Mr. Noah. "That's all. Your tears are dry on me now. Good-bye." And he laid down his yellow mat, stepped onto it, and was just a little wooden figure again.

Philip dropped the ear trumpet and looked at Mr. Noah.

"I *don't* understand," he said. But this at least he understood. That Helen would come back when she got that telegram, and that before she came he must go into the other world and find the lost Lucy.

"But, oh," he said, "suppose I *don't* find her. I wish I hadn't built those cities so big! And time will go on. And, perhaps, when Helen comes back she'll find *me* lost *too*—as well as Lucy."

But he dried his eyes and told himself that this was not how heroes behaved. He must build again. Whichever way you looked at it there was no time to be lost. And besides, the nurse might occur at any moment.

He looked around for building materials. There was the chess table. It had long narrow legs set round it, rather like arches. Something might be done with it, with books and candlesticks and Japanese vases.

Something *was* done. Philip built with earnest care, but also with considerable speed. If the nurse should come in before he had made a door and gotten through it—come in and find him building again—she was quite capable of putting him to bed, where, of course, building is impossible. In a very little time there was a building. But how to get in? He was, alas, the wrong size. He stood helpless, and once more tears pricked and swelled behind his eyelids. One tear fell on his hand.

"Tears are a strong magic," Mr. Noah had said. And at the thought the tears stopped. Still there *was* a tear, the one on his hand. He rubbed it on the pillar of the porch.

And instantly a queer, tight, thin feeling swept through him. He felt giddy and shut his eyes. His boots, ever sympathetic, shuffled on the carpet. Or was it the carpet? It was very thick and—he opened his eyes. His feet were once more on the long grass of the illimitable prairie. And in front of him towered the gigantic porch of a vast building and a domino path leading up to it.

"Oh, I am so glad," cried Philip among the grass. "I couldn't have borne it if she'd been lost forever, and all my fault."

The gigantic porch lowered frowningly above him. What would he find on the other side of it?

"I don't care. I've simply got to go," he said, and stepped out bravely. "If I can't *be* a hero I'll try to behave like one."

And with that he stepped out, stumbling a little in the thick grass, and the dark shadow of the porch received him.

"Bother the child," said the nurse, coming into the drawing room a little later, "if he hasn't been at his precious building game again! I shall have to give him a lesson over this—I can see that. And I will too—a lesson he won't forget in a hurry."

*The gigantic porch lowered frowningly above him.*

She went through the house, looking for the too bold builder, that she might give him that lesson. Then she went through the garden, still on the same errand.

Half an hour later she burst into the servants' hall and threw herself into a chair.

"I don't care what happens now," she said. "The house is bewitched, I think. I shall go the very minute I've had my dinner."

"What's up now?" the cook came to the door to say.

"Up?" said the nurse. "Oh, nothing's *up*. What should there be? Everything's all right and beautiful, and just as it should be, of course."

"Miss Lucy's not found yet, of course, but that's all, isn't it?"

"All? And enough too, I should have thought," said the nurse. "But as it happens it's *not* all. The boy's lost now. Oh, I'm not joking. He's lost I tell you, the same as the other one—and I'm off out of this by the two thirty-seven train, and I don't care who knows it."

"Lor'!" said the cook.


Before starting for the two thirty-seven train the nurse went back to the drawing room to destroy Philip's new building, to restore to their proper places its books, candlesticks, vases, and chessmen.

There we will leave her.

## CHAPTER FOUR

# The Dragon Slayer

WHEN PHILIP walked up the domino path and under the vast arch
into the darkness beyond, his heart felt strong with high resolve. His
legs, however, felt weak; strangely weak, especially about the knees.
The doorway was so enormous, that which lay beyond was so dark,
and he himself so very, very small. As he passed under the little gateway that he had built of three dominoes with the little silver knight in
armor on the top, he noticed that he was only as high as a domino,
and you know how very little that is.

Philip went along the domino path. He had to walk carefully, for
to him the spots on the dominoes were quite deep hollows. But as they
were black they were easy to see. He had made three arches, one
beyond another, of two pairs of silver candlesticks with silver inkstands on the top of them. The third pair of silver candlesticks had a
book on the top of them because there were no more inkstands. And
when he had passed through the three silver arches, he stopped.

Beyond lay a sort of velvety darkness with white gleams in it. And
as his eyes became accustomed to the darkness, he saw that he was in
a great hall of silver pillars, gigantic silver candlesticks they seemed to
be, and they went in long vistas this way and that way and every way,

like the hop poles in a hop field, so that whichever way you turned, a long pillared corridor lay in front of you.

Philip had no idea which way he ought to go. It seemed most unlikely that he would find Lucy in a dark hall with silver pillars.

"All the same," he said, "it's not so dark as it was, by long chalks."

It was not. The silver pillars had begun to give out a faint soft glow like the silver phosphorescence that lies in sea pools in summertime.

"It's lucky too," he said, "because of the holes in the floor."

The holes were the spots on the dominoes with which the pillared hall was paved.

"I wonder what part of the city where Lucy is I shall come out at?" Philip asked himself. But he need not have troubled. He did not come out at all. He walked on and on and on and on and on. He thought he was walking straight, but really he was turning first this way and then that, and then the other way among the avenues of silver pillars which all looked just alike.

He was getting very tired, and he had been walking a long time, before he came to anything that was not silver pillars and velvet black under invisible roofs, and floor paved with dominoes laid very close together.

"Oh, I am glad!" he said at last, when he saw the pavement narrow to a single line of dominoes just like the path he had come in by. There was an arch too, like the arch by which he had come in. And then he perceived in a shock of miserable surprise that it was, in fact, the same arch and the same domino path. He had come back, after all that walking, to the point from which he had started. It was most mortifying. So silly! Philip sat down on the edge of the domino path to rest and think.

"Suppose I just walk out and don't believe in magic anymore?" he said to himself. "Helen says magic can only happen to people who believe in magic. So if I just walked out and didn't believe as hard as ever I could, I should be my own right size again, and Lucy would be back, and there wouldn't *be* any magic."

*He walked on and on and on.*

"Yes, but," said that voice that always would come and join in whenever Philip was talking to himself, "suppose Lucy *does* believe it? Then it'll all go on for her, whatever *you* believe, and she *won't* be back. Besides, you know you've *got* to believe it, because it's true."

"Oh, bother!" said Philip. "I'm tired. I don't want to go on."

"You shouldn't have deserted Lucy," said the tiresome voice, "then you wouldn't have had to go back to look for her."

"But I can't find my way. How can I find my way?"

"You know well enough. Fix your eyes on a far-off pillar and walk straight to it, and when you're nearly there fix your eyes a little farther. You're bound to come out somewhere."

"But I'm tired and it's so lonely," said Philip.

"Lucy's lonely too," said the voice.

"Drop it!" said Philip. And he got up and began to walk again. Also he took the advice of that worrying voice and fixed his eyes on a distant pillar.

"But why should I bother?" he said. "This is a sort of dream."

"Even if it *were* a dream," said the voice, "there are adventures in it. So you may as well be adventurous."

"Oh, all right," said Philip, and on he went.

And by walking very carefully and fixing his eyes a long way off, he did at last come right through the hall of silver pillars, and saw beyond the faint glow of the pillars the blue light of day. It shone very brightly through a very little door, and when Philip came to that door he went through it without hesitation. And there he was in a big field. It was rather like the illimitable prairie, only there were great patches of different-colored flowers. Also there was a path across it, and he followed the path.

"Because," he said, "I'm more likely to meet Lucy. Girls always keep to paths. They never explore."

Which just shows how little he knew about girls.

He looked back after a while, to see what the hall of pillars looked like from outside, but it was already dim in the mists of distance.

But ahead of him he saw a great rough building, rather like Stonehenge.

"I wish I'd come into the other city where the people are, and the soldiers, and the greyhounds, and the coconuts," he told himself. "There's nobody here at all, not even Lucy."

The loneliness of the place grew more and more unpleasing to Philip. But he went on. It seemed more reasonable than to go back.

"I ought to be very hungry," he said. "I must have been walking for hours." But he wasn't hungry. It may have been the magic, or it may have been the odd breakfast he had had. I don't know. He spoke aloud because it was so quiet in that strange open country with no one in it but himself. And no sound but the clump, clump of his boots on the path. And it seemed to him that everything grew quieter and quieter till he could almost hear himself think. Loneliness, real loneliness is a dreadful thing. I hope you will never feel it. Philip looked to right and left, and before him, and on all the wide plain nothing moved. There were the grass and flowers, but no wind stirred them. And there was no sign that any living person had ever trodden that path—except that there *was* a path to tread, and that the path led to the Stonehenge building, and even that seemed to be only a ruin.

"I'll go as far as that anyhow," said Philip. "Perhaps there'll be a signboard there or something."

There was something. Something most unexpected. Philip reached the building; it was really very like Stonehenge, only the pillars were taller and closer together and there was one high solid towering wall; turned the corner of a massive upright, and ran almost into the arms, and quite onto the feet, of a man in a white apron and a square paper cap, who sat on a fallen column, eating bread and cheese with a clasp knife.

"I beg your pardon!" Philip gasped.

"Granted, I'm sure," said the man, "but it's a dangerous thing to do, Master Philip, running sheer onto chaps' clasp knives."

He set Philip on his feet, and waved the knife, which had been so often sharpened that the blade was half worn away.

"Set you down and get your breath," he said kindly.

"Why, it's *you*!" said Philip.

"Course it is. Who should I be if I wasn't me? That's poetry."

"But how did you get here?"

"Ah!" said the man, going on with his bread and cheese, while he talked quite in the friendliest way. "That's telling."

"Well, tell then," said Philip impatiently. But he sat down.

"Well, you say it's me. Who be it? Give it a name."

"You're old Perrin," said Pip. "I mean, of course, I beg your pardon, you're Mr. Perrin, the carpenter."

"And what does carpenters do?"

"Carp, I suppose," said Philip. "That means they make things, doesn't it?"

"That's it," said the man encouragingly. "What sort of things now might old Perrin have made for you?"

"You made my wheelbarrow, I know," said Philip, "and my bricks."

"Ah!" said Mr. Perrin. "Now you've got it. I made your bricks, seasoned oak, and true to the thousandth of an inch, they was. And that's how I got here. So now you know."

"But what are you doing here?" said Philip, wriggling restlessly on the fallen column.

"Waiting for you. Them as knows sent me out to meet you, and give you a hint of what's expected of you."

"Well. What *is*?" said Philip. "I mean I think it's very kind of you. What *is* expected?"

"Plenty of time," said the carpenter, "plenty. Nothing ain't expected of you till toward sundown."

"I do think it was most awfully kind of you," said Philip, who had now thought this over.

"You was kind to old Perrin once," said that person.

"Was I?" said Philip, much surprised.

"Yes; when my little girl was ailing you brought her a lot of pears off your own tree. Not one of 'em you didn't 'ave yourself that year, Miss Helen told me. And you brought back our kitten—the sandy and white one with black spots—when it strayed. So I was quite willing to come and meet you when so told. And knowing something of young gentlemen's peckers, owing to being in business once next door to a boys' school, I made so bold as to bring you a snack."

He reached a hand down behind the fallen pillar on which they sat and brought up a basket.

"Here," he said. And Philip, raising the lid, was delighted to find that he was hungry. It was a pleasant basketful. Meat pasties, red hairy gooseberries, a stone bottle of ginger beer, a blue mug with "Philip" on it in gold letters, a slice of soda cake, and two farthing sugar-sticks.

"I'm sure I've seen that basket before," said the boy as he ate.

"Like enough. It's the one you brought them pears down in."

"Now, look here," said Philip, through his seventh bite of pasty, "you *must* tell me how you got here. And tell me where you've got to. You've simply no idea how muddling it all is to me. Do tell me *everything*. Where are we, I mean, and why? And what I've got to do. And why? And when? Tell me every single thing." And he took the eighth bite.

"You really don't know, sir?"

"No," said Philip, contemplating the ninth or last bite but one. It was a large pasty.

"Well then. Here goes. But I was always a poor speaker, and so considered even by friends at cricket dinners and what not."

"But I don't want you to speak," said Philip. "Just tell me."

"Well, then. How did I get here? I got here through having made them bricks what you built this tumbledown old ancient place with."

"*I* built?"

"Yes, with them bricks I made you. I understand as this was the first building you ever put up. That's why it's first on the road to where you want to get to!"

Philip looked round at the Stonehenge building and saw that it was indeed built of enormous oak bricks.

"Of course," he said, "only I've grown smaller."

"Or they've grown bigger," said Mr. Perrin. "It's the same thing. You see it's like this. All the cities and things you ever built is in this country. I don't know how it's managed, no more'n what you do. But so it is. And as you made 'em, you've the right to come to them—if you can get there. And you have got there. It isn't everyone has the luck, I'm told. Well, then, you made the cities, but you made 'em out of what other folks had made, things like bricks and chessmen and books and candlesticks and dominoes and brass basins and every sort of kind of thing. An' all the people who helped to make all them things you used to build with, they're all here too. D'you see? *Making's* the thing. If it was no more than the lad that turned the handle of the grindstone to sharp the knife that carved a bit of a cabinet or what not, or a child that picked a teazle to finish a bit of the cloth that's glued on to the bottom of a chessman—they're all here. They're what's called the population of your cities."

"I see. They've got small, like I have," said Philip.

"Or the cities has got big," said the carpenter. "It comes to the same thing. I wish you wouldn't interrupt, Master Philip. You put me out."

"I won't again," said Philip. "Only do tell me just one thing. How can you be here and at Amblehurst too?"

"We come here," said the carpenter slowly, "when we're asleep."

"Oh!" said Philip, deeply disappointed. "It's just a dream, then?"

"Not it. We come here when we're too sound asleep to dream. You go through the dreams and come out on the other side where everything's real. That's *here*."

"Go on," said Philip.

"I dunno where I was. You do put me out so."

"Pop you something or other," said Philip.

"Population. Yes. Well, all those people as made the things you made the cities of, they live in the cities and they've made the insides to the houses."

"What do they do?"

"Oh, they just live here. And they buy and sell and plant gardens and work and play like everybody does in other cities. And when they go to sleep they go slap through their dreams and into the other world, and work and play there, see? That's how it goes on. There's a lot more, but that's enough for one time. You get on with your gooseberries."

"But they aren't all real people, are they? There's Mr. Noah?"

"Ah, those is aristocracy, the ones you put in when you built the cities. They're our old families. Very much respected. They're all very high up in the world. Came over with the Conker, as the saying is. There's the Noah family. They're the oldest of all, of course. And the dolls you've put in different times and the tin soldiers, and of course all the Noah's ark animals is alive except when you used them for building, and then they're statues."

"But I don't see," said Philip, "I really don't see how all these cities that I built at different times can still be here, all together and all going on at once, when I know they've all been pulled down."

"Well, I'm no scholard. But I did hear Mr. Noah say once in a lecture—*he's* a speaker, if you like—I heard him say it was like when you take a person's photo. The person is so many inches thick through and so many feet high and he's round and he's solid. But in the photo he's *flat.* Because everything's flat in photos. But all the same it's him right enough. You get him into the photo. Then all you've got to do is to get 'im out again into where everything's thick and tall and round and solid. And it's quite easy, I believe, once you know the trick."

"Stop," said Philip suddenly. "I think my head's going to burst."

"Ah!" said the carpenter kindly. "I felt like that at first. Lie down and try to sleep it off a bit. Eddication does go to your head something crool. I've often noticed it."

And indeed Philip was quite glad to lie down among the long grass and be covered up with the carpenter's coat. He fell asleep at once.

An hour later he woke again, looked at the wrinkled-apple face of Mr. Perrin, and began to remember.

"I'm glad *you're* here anyhow," he said to the carpenter. "It was horribly lonely. You don't know."

"That's why I was sent to meet you," said Mr. Perrin simply.

"But how did you know?"

"Mr. Noah sent for me early this morning. Bless you, he knows all about everything. Says he, 'You go and meet 'im and tell 'im all you can. If he wants to be a Deliverer, let 'im,' says Mr. Noah."

"But how do you begin being a Deliverer?" Philip asked, sitting up and feeling suddenly very grand and manly, and very glad that Lucy was not there to interfere.

"There's lots of different ways," said Mr. Perrin. "Your particular way's simple. You just got to kill the dragon."

"A *live* dragon?"

"Live!" said Mr. Perrin. "Why, he's all over the place and as green as grass he is. Lively as a kitten. He's got a broken spear sticking out of his side, so someone must have had a try at baggin' him, sometime or another."

"Don't you think," said Philip, a little overcome by this vivid picture, "that perhaps I'd better look for Lucy first, and be a Deliverer afterward?"

"If you're *afraid*," said Mr. Perrin.

"I'm not," said Philip doubtfully.

"You see," said the carpenter, "what you've got to consider is: are you going to be the hero of this 'ere adventure or ain't you? You can't 'ave it both ways. An' if you are, you may's well make up your mind, cause killing a dragon ain't the end of it, not by no means."

"Do you mean there are more dragons?"

"Not dragons," said the carpenter soothingly, "not dragons exactly. But there. I don't want to lower your heart. If you kills the dragon, then afterward there's six more hard things you've got to do. And then they make you king. Take it or leave it. Only, if you take it we'd best be starting. And anyhow we may as well get a move on us, because at sundown the dragon comes out to drink and exercise of himself. You can hear him rattling all night among these 'ere ruins; miles off you can 'ear 'im of a still night."

"Suppose I don't want to be a Deliverer," said Philip slowly.

"Then you'll be a Destroyer," said the carpenter. "There's only these two situations vacant here at present. Come, Master Philip, sir, don't talk as if you wasn't going to be a man and do your duty for England, Home, and Beauty, like it says in the song. Let's be starting, shall us?"

"You think I ought to be the Deliverer?"

"Ought stands for nothing," said Mr. Perrin. I think you're a going to *be* the Deliverer; that's what I think. Come on!"

As they rose to go, Philip had a brief fleeting vision of a very smart lady in a motor veil, disappearing round the corner of a pillar.

"Are there many motors about here?" he asked, not wishing to talk any more about dragons just then.

"Not a single one," said Mr. Perrin unexpectedly. "Nor yet phonographs, nor railways, nor factory chimneys, nor none of them loud ugly things. Nor yet advertisements, nor newspapers, nor barbed wire."

After that the two walked silently away from the ruin. Philip was trying to feel as brave and confident as a Deliverer should. He reminded himself of St. George. And he remembered that the hero *never* fails to kill the dragon. But he still felt a little uneasy. It takes some time to accustom yourself to being a hero. But he could not help looking over his shoulder every now and then to see if the dragon was coming. So far it wasn't.

"Well," said Mr. Perrin as they drew near a square tower with a long flight of steps leading up to it, "what do you say?"

"I wasn't saying anything," said Philip.

"I mean are you going to be the Deliverer?"

Then something in Philip's heart seemed to swell, and a choking feeling came into his throat, and he felt more frightened than he had ever felt before, as he said, looking as brave as he could:

"Yes. I am."

Perrin clapped his hands.

And instantly from the doors of the tower and from behind it came dozens of people, and down the long steps, alone, came Mr. Noah, moving with careful dignity and carrying his yellow mat neatly rolled under his arm. All the people clapped their hands, till Mr. Noah, standing on the third step, raised his hands to command silence.

"Friends," he said, "and fellow citizens of Polistopolis, you see before you one who says that he is the Deliverer. He was yesterday arrested and tried as a trespasser, and condemned to imprisonment. He escaped and you all assumed that he was the Destroyer in disguise. But now he has returned and of his own free will he chooses to attempt the accomplishment of the seven great deeds. And the first of these is the killing of the great green dragon."

The people, who were a mixed crowd of all nations, cheered loudly.

"So now," said Mr. Noah, "we will make him our knight."

"Kneel," said Mr. Noah, "in token of fealty to the Kingdom of Cities."

Philip knelt.

"You shall now speak after me," said Mr. Noah solemnly. "Say what I say," he whispered, and Philip said it.

This was it. "I, Philip, claim to be the Deliverer of this great nation, and I pledge myself to carry out the seven great deeds that shall prove my claim to the Delivership and the throne. I pledge my honor to be the champion of this city, and the enemy of its Destroyer."

When Philip had said this, Mr. Noah drew forth a bright silver-hilted sword and held it over him.

"You must be knighted," he said. "Those among my audience who have read any history will be aware that no mere commoner can expect to conquer a dragon. We must give our would-be Deliverer every chance. So I will make him a knight." He tapped Philip lightly on the shoulder and said, "Rise up, Sir Philip!"

This was really grand, and Philip felt new courage as Mr. Noah handed him the silver sword, and all the people cheered.

But as the cheers died down, a thin and disagreeable voice suddenly said:

"But *I* claim to be the Deliverer too."

It was like a thunderbolt. Everyone stopped cheering and stood with mouth open and head turned toward the person who had spoken. And the person who had spoken was the smartly dressed lady in the motor veil, whom Philip had seen among the ruins.

"A trespasser! A trespasser!" cried the crowd. "To prison with it!" And angry, threatening voices began to arise.

"I'm no more a trespasser than he is," said the voice, "and if I say I am the Deliverer, you can't stop me. I can kill dragons or do anything *he* can do."

"Silence, trespasser," said Mr. Noah, with cold dignity. "You should have spoken earlier. At present Sir Philip occupies the position of candidate to the post of King-Deliverer. There is no other position open to you except that of Destroyer."

"But suppose the boy doesn't do it?" said the voice behind the veil.

"True," said Mr. Noah. "You may if you choose, occupy for the present the position of Pretender-in-Chief to the Claimancy of the Deliverership, an office now and here created expressly for you. The position of Claimant to the Destroyership is also," he added reflectively, "open to you."

"Then if he doesn't do it," said the veiled lady, "I can be the Deliverer."

"You can try," said Mr. Noah. "There are a special set of tasks to be performed if the claimant to the Deliverership be a woman."

"What are they?" said the veiled lady.

"If Sir Philip fails you will be duly instructed in the deeds required of a Deliverer who is a woman. And now, my friends, let us retire and

*"Silence, trespasser,"* said Mr. Noah, with cold dignity.

leave Sir Philip to deal with the dragon. We shall watch anxiously from yonder ramparts," he added encouragingly.

"But isn't anyone to help me?" said Philip, deeply uneasy.

"It is not usual," said Mr. Noah, "for champions to require assistance with dragons."

"I should think not indeed," said the veiled lady, "but you're not going the usual way about it at all. Where's the princess, I should like to know?"

"There isn't any princess," said Mr. Noah.

"Then it won't be a proper dragon killing," she said, with an angry shaking of skirts, "that's all I can say."

"I wish it *was* all," said Mr. Noah to himself.

"If there isn't a princess it isn't fair," said the veiled one, "and I shall consider it's my turn to be Deliverer."

"Be silent, woman," said Mr. Noah.

"Woman, indeed," said the lady. "I ought to have a proper title."

"Your title is the Pretender to the—"

"I know," she interrupted, "but you forget you're speaking to a lady. You can call me the Pretenderette."

Mr. Noah turned coldly from her and pressed two Roman candles and a box of matches into Philip's hand.

"When you have arranged your plans and are quite sure that you will be able to kill the dragon, light one of these. We will then have a princess in readiness, and on observing your signal will tie her to a tree, or, since this is a district where trees are rare and buildings frequent, to a pillar. She will be perfectly safe if you make your plans correctly. And in any case you must not attempt to deal with the dragon without first lighting the Roman candle."

"And the dragon will see it and go away."

"Exactly," said Mr. Noah. "Or perhaps he will see it and not go away. Time alone will show. The task that is without difficulties can never really appeal to a hero. You will find weapons, cords, nets, shields, and various first aids to the young Dragon-Catcher in the vaults below this tower. Good evening, Sir Philip," he ended warmly. "We wish you every success."

And with that the whole crowd began to go away.

"*I* know who you ought to have for Princess," the Pretenderette said as they went. And Mr. Noah said:

"Silence in court."

"This isn't a court," said the Pretenderette aggravatingly.

"Wherever justice is, is a court," said Mr. Noah, "and I accuse you of contempt of it. Guards, arrest this person and take her to prison at once."

There was a scuffling and a shrieking and then the voices withdrew gradually, the angry voice of even the Pretenderette growing fainter and fainter till it died away altogether.

Philip was left alone.

His first act was to go up to the top of the tower and look out to see if he could see the dragon. He looked east and north and south and west, and he saw the ramparts of the fort where Mr. Noah and the others were now safely bestowed. He saw also other towers and cities in the distance, and he saw the ruins where he had met Mr. Perrin.

And among those ruins something was moving. Something long and jointed and green. It could be nothing but the dragon.

"Oh, crikey!" said Philip to himself. "Whatever shall I do? Perhaps I'd better see what weapons there are."

So he ran down the stairs and down and down till he came to the vaults of the castle, and there he found everything a dragon-killer could possibly need, even to a little red book called the *Young Dragon-Catcher's Vade Mecum, or A Complete Guide to the Good Sport of Dragon Slaying*, and a pair of excellent field glasses.

The top of the tower seemed the safest place. It was there that he tried to read the book. The words were very long and most difficultly spelled. But he did manage to make out that all dragons sleep for one hour after sunset. Then he heard a loud rattling sound from the ruin, and he knew it was the dragon who was making that sound, so he looked through the field glasses, frowning with anxiety to see what the dragon was doing.

And as he looked he started and almost dropped the glasses, and the frown cleared away from his forehead and he gave a sigh that was almost a sob and almost a laugh, and then he said:

"That old thing!"

Then he looked again, and this is what he saw. An enormous green dragon, very long and fierce-looking, that rattled as it moved, going in and out among the ruins, rubbing itself against the fallen pillars. And the reason Philip laughed and sighed was that he knew that dragon very well indeed. He had known it long ago. It was the clockwork lizard that had been given him the Christmas before last. And he remembered that he had put it into one of the cities he and Helen had built together. Only now, of course, it had grown big and had come alive like all the other images of live things he had put in his cities. But he saw that it was still a clockwork creature. And its key was sticking out of its side. And it was rubbing itself against the pillars so as to turn the key and wind itself up. But this was a slow business and the winding was not half done when the sun set. The dragon instantly lay down and went to sleep.

"Well," said Philip, "now I've got to think."

He did think, harder than he had ever done before. And when he had finished thinking he went down into the vault and got a long rope. Then he stood still a moment, wondering if he really were brave enough. And then he remembered "Rise up, Sir Philip," and he knew that a knight simply *mustn't* be afraid.

So he went out in the dusk toward the dragon.

He knew it would sleep for an hour. But all the same—and the twilight was growing deeper and deeper. Still there was plenty of light to find the ruin, and also to find the dragon. There it lay—about ten or twelve yards of solid dark dragon flesh. Its metal claws gleamed in the last of the daylight. Its great mouth was open, and its breathing, as it slept, was like the sound of the sea on a rough night.

"Rise up, Sir Philip," he said to himself, and walked along close to the dragon till he came to the middle part where the key was sticking out—which Mr. Perrin had thought was a piece of an old spear with which someone had once tried to kill the monster.

Philip fastened one end of his rope very securely to the key—how thankful he was that Helen had taught him to tie knots that were not granny knots. The dragon lay quite still, and went on breathing like a stormy sea. Then the dragon-slayer fastened the other end of the rope to the main wall of the ruin, which was very strong and firm, and then he went back to his tower as fast as he could and struck a match and lighted his Roman candle.

You see the idea? It was really rather a clever one. When the dragon woke it would find that it was held prisoner by the ropes. It would be furious and try to get free. And in its struggles it would be certain to get free, but this it could only do by detaching itself from its key. When once the key was out the dragon would be unable to wind itself up anymore, and would be as good as dead. Of course Sir Philip could cut off its head with the silver-hilted sword if Mr. Noah really wished it.

It was, as you see, an excellent plan, as far as it went. Philip sat on the top of his tower quite free from anxiety, and ate a few hairy red gooseberries that happened to be loose in his pocket. Within three minutes of his lighting his Roman candle a shower of golden rain went up in the south, some immense Catherine wheels appeared in the east, and in the north a long line of rockets presented almost the appearance of an aurora borealis. Red fire, green fire, then rockets again. The whole of the plain was lit by more fireworks than Philip had ever seen, even at the Crystal Palace. By their light he saw a procession come out of the fort, cross to a pillar that stood solitary on the plain, and tie to it a white figure.

"The Princess, I suppose," said Philip. "Well, *she's* all right, anyway."

Then the procession went back to the fort, and then the dragon awoke. Philip could see the great creature stretching itself and shaking its vast head as a dog does when it comes out of the water.

"I expect it doesn't like the fireworks," said Philip. And he was quite right.

And now the dragon saw the Princess who had been placed at a convenient spot about halfway between the ruins and Philip's tower.

It threw up its snout and uttered a devastating howl, and Philip felt with a thrill of horror that clockwork or no clockwork, the brute was alive, and desperately dangerous.

And now it had perceived that it was bound. With great heavings and throes, with snortings and bellowings, with scratchings and tearings of its great claws and lashings of its terrible tail, it writhed and fought to be free, and the light of thousands of fireworks illuminated the gigantic struggle.

Then what Philip had known would happen did happen. The great wall held fast, the rope held fast, the dragon held fast. It was the key that gave way. With an echoing, grinding, rusty sound like a goods train shunting on a siding, the key was drawn from the keyhole in the dragon's side and left still fast to its rope like an anchor to a cable.

*Left.* For now that happened which Philip had not foreseen. He had forgotten that before it fell asleep the dragon had partly wound itself up. And its struggles had not used up all the winding. There was go in the dragon yet. And with a yell of fury it set off across the plain, wriggling its green rattling length toward—the Princess.

And now there was no time to think whether one was afraid or not. Philip went down those tower stairs more quickly than he had ever gone down stairs in his life, and he was not bad at stairs even at ordinary times.

He put his sword over his shoulder as you do a gun, and ran. Like the dragon he made straight for the Princess. And now it was a race between him and the dragon. Philip ran and ran. His heart thumped; his feet had that leaden feeling that comes in nightmares. He felt as if he were dying.

Keep on, keep on, faster, faster, you mustn't stop. Ah! That's better.

He has got his second wind. He is going faster. And the dragon—or is it fancy?—is going not quite so fast.

How he did it Philip never knew. But with a last spurt he reached the pillar where the Princess stood bound. And the dragon was twenty yards away, coming on and on and on.

Philip stood quite still, recovering his breath. And more and more slowly, but with no sign of stopping, the dragon came on. Behind him, where the pillar was, Philip heard someone crying softly.

Then the dragon was quite near. Philip took three steps forward, took aim with his sword, shut his eyes and hit as hard as he could. Then something hard and heavy knocked him over, and for a time he knew no more.

When he came to himself again, Mr. Noah was giving him something nasty to drink out of a medicine glass, Mr. Perrin was patting him on the back, all the people were shouting like mad, and more fireworks than ever were being let off. Beside him lay the dragon, lifeless and still.

"Oh!" said Philip. "Did I really do it?"

"You did indeed," said Mr. Noah, "however you may succeed with the other deeds, you are the hero of this one. And now, if you feel well enough, prepare to receive the reward of Valor and Chivalry."

"Oh!" said Philip, brightening. "I didn't know there was to be a reward."

"Only the usual one," said Mr. Noah. "The Princess, you know."

Philip became aware that a figure in a white veil was standing quite near him; around its feet lay lengths of cut rope.

"The Princess is yours," said Mr. Noah, with generous affability.

"But I don't want her," said Philip, adding by an afterthought, "thank you."

"You should have thought of that before," said Mr. Noah. "You can't go doing deeds of valor, you know, and then shirking the reward. Take her. She is yours."

*Then something hard and heavy knocked him over.*

"Anyone who likes may have her," said Philip desperately. "If she's mine, I can give her away, can't I? You must see yourself I can't be bothered with princesses if I've got all those other deeds to do."

"That's not my affair," said Mr. Noah. "Perhaps you might arrange to board her out while you're doing your deeds. But at present she is waiting for you to take her by the hand and raise her veil."

"Must I?" said Philip miserably. "Well, here goes."

He took a small cold hand in one of his and with the other lifted, very gingerly, a corner of the veil. The other hand of the Princess drew back the veil, and the Dragon-Slayer and the Princess were face-to-face.

"Why!" cried Philip, between relief and disgust. "It's only Lucy!"

## CHAPTER FIVE

# On the Carpet

THE PRINCESS was just Lucy. "It's too bad," said Philip. "I do think." Then he stopped short and just looked cross.

"The Princess and the Champion will now have their teas," said Mr. Noah. "Right about face, everybody, please, and quick march."

Philip and Lucy found themselves marching side by side through the night made yellow with continuous fireworks.

You must picture them marching across a great plain of grass where many colored flowers grew. You see, a good many of Philip's buildings had been made on the drawing room carpet at home, which was green with pink and blue and yellow and white flowers. And this carpet had turned into grass and growing flowers, following that strange law which caused things to change into other things, like themselves, but larger and really belonging to a living world.

No one spoke. Philip said nothing because he was in a bad temper. And if you are in a bad temper, nothing is a good thing to say. To circumvent a dragon and then kill it, and to have such an adventure end in tea with Lucy, was too much. And he had other reasons for silence too. And Lucy was silent because she had so much to say that she didn't know where to begin, and besides, she could feel how cross

Philip was. The crowd did not talk because it was not etiquette to talk when taking part in processions. Mr. Noah did not talk because it made him out of breath to walk and talk at the same time, two things neither of which he had been designed to do.

So that it was quite a silent party which at last passed through the gateway of the town and up its streets.

Philip wondered where the tea would be—not in the prison of course. It was very late for tea too, quite the middle of the night it seemed. But all the streets were brilliantly lighted, and flags and festoons of flowers hung from all the windows and across all the streets.

It was in the front of a big building in one of the great squares of the city that an extra display of colored lamps disclosed open doors and red-carpeted steps. Mr. Noah hurried up them, and turned to receive Philip and Lucy.

"The City of Polistopolis," he said, "whose unworthy representative I am, greets in my person the most noble Sir Philip, Knight and Slayer of the Dragon. Also the Princess whom he has rescued. Be pleased to enter."

They went up the red cloth-covered steps and into a hall, very splendid with silver and ivory. Mr. Noah stooped to a confidential question.

"You'd like a wash, perhaps?" he said. "And your Princess too. And perhaps you'd like to dress up a little? Before the banquet, you know."

"Banquet?" said Philip. "I thought it was tea."

"Business before pleasure," said Mr. Noah. "First the banquet, then the tea. This way to the dressing rooms."

There were two doors side by side. On one door was painted "Knight's dressing room," on the other, "Princess's dressing room."

"Look out," said Mr. Noah, "the paint is wet. You see, there wasn't much time."

Philip found his dressing room very interesting. The walls were entirely of looking glass, and on tables in the middle of the room lay all sorts of clothes of beautiful colors and odd shapes. Shoes, stockings, hats, crowns, armor, swords, cloaks, breeches, waistcoats, jerkins, trunk hose. An open door showed a marble bathroom. The bath was sunk in the floor as the baths of luxurious Roman empresses used to be, and as nowadays baths sometimes are in model dwellings. (Only I am told that some people keep their coals in the baths—which is quite useless because coals are always black however much you wash them.)

Philip undressed and went into the warm clear water, greenish between the air and the marble. Why is it so pleasant to have a bath, and so tiresome to wash your hands and face in a basin? He put on his shirt and knickerbockers again, and wandered round the room looking at the clothes laid out there, and wondering which of the wonderful costumes would be really suitable for a knight to wear at a banquet. After considerable hesitation he decided on a little soft shirt of chain mail that made just a double handful of tiny steel links as he held it. But a difficulty arose.

"I don't know how to put it on," said Philip, "and I expect the banquet is waiting. How cross it'll be."

He stood undecided, holding the chain mail in his hands, when his eyes fell on a bell handle. Above it was an ivory plate, and on it in black letters the word "Valet." Philip rang the bell.

Instantly, a soft tap at the door heralded the entrance of a person whom Philip at the first glance supposed to be a sandwich man. But the second glance showed that the oblong flat things that he wore were not sandwich boards, but dominoes. The person between them bowed low.

"Oh!" said Philip. "I rang for the valet."

"I am not the valet," said the domino-enclosed person, who seemed to be in skintight black clothes under his dominoes, "I am the Master of the Robes. I only attend on really distinguished persons. Double-six, at your service, sir. Have you chosen your dress?"

"I'd like to wear the armor," said Philip, holding it out. "It seems the right thing for a Knight," he added.

"Quite so, sir. I confirm your opinion."

He proceeded to dress Philip in a white tunic and to fasten the coat of mail over this. "I've had a great deal of experience," he said. "You couldn't have chosen better. You see, I'm master of the subject of dress. I am able to give my whole mind to it; my own dress being fixed by law and not subject to changes of fashion leaves me free to think for others. And I think deeply. But I see that you can think for yourself."

You have no idea how jolly Philip looked in the mail coat and mailed hood—just like a Crusader.

At the doorway of the dressing room he met Lucy in a short white dress and a coronal of pearls round her head. "I always wanted to be a fairy," she said.

"Did you have anyone to dress you?" he asked.

"Oh no!" said Lucy calmly. "I always dress myself."

"Ladies have the advantage there," said Double-six, bowing and walking backward. "The banquet is spread."

It turned out to be spread on three tables, one along each side of a great room, and one across the top of the room, on a dais—such a table as that high one at which dons and distinguished strangers sit in the halls of colleges.

Mr. Noah was already in his place in the middle of the high table, and Lucy and Philip now took their places at each side of him. The table was spread with all sorts of nice-looking foods and plates of a pink-and-white pattern very familiar to Philip. They were, in fact, as he soon realized, the painted wooden plates from his sister's old doll-house. There was no food just in front of the children, only a great empty bowl of silver.

Philip fingered his knife and fork; the pattern of those also was familiar to him. They were indeed the little leaden ones out of the doll-house knife basket of green and silver filigree. He hungrily waited. Servants in straight yellow dresses and red masks and caps were beginning to handle the dishes. A dish was handed to him. A beautiful jelly it looked like. He took up his spoon and was just about to help himself, when Mr. Noah whispered ardently, "Don't!" and as Philip looked at him in astonishment he added, still in a whisper, "Pretend, can't you? Have you never had a pretending banquet?" But before he had caught the whisper, Philip had tried to press the edge of the leaden spoon into the shape of jelly. And he felt that the jelly was quite hard. He went through the form of helping himself, but it was just nothing that he put on his plate. And he saw that Mr. Noah and Lucy and all the other guests did the same. Presently another dish was handed to him. There was no changing of plates. "They *needn't*," Philip thought bitterly. This time it was a fat goose, not carved, and now Philip saw that it was attached to its dish with glue. Then he understood.

(You know the beautiful but uneatable feasts that are given you in a white cardboard box with blue binding and fine shavings to pack the dishes and keep them from breaking? I myself, when I was little, had such a banquet in a box. There were twelve dishes: a ham, brown and shapely; a pair of roast chickens, also brown and more anatomical than the ham; a glazed tongue, real tongue-shape, none of your tinned round mysteries; a dish of sausages; two handsome fish, a little blue, perhaps; a joint of beef, ribs I think, very red as to the lean and very white in the fat parts; a pork pie, delicately bronzed like a traveler in Central Africa. For sweets I had shapes, shapes of beauty, a jelly and a cream; a Swiss roll too, and a plum pudding; asparagus there was also and a cauliflower, and a dish of the greenest peas in all this gray world. This was my banquet outfit. I remember that the woodenness of it all depressed us wonderfully; the oneness of dish and food baffled all make-believe. With the point of nurse's scissors we pried the viands from the platters. But their wooden nature was unconquerable. One could not pretend to eat a whole chicken any better when it was detached from its dish, and the sausages were one solid block. And when you licked the jelly it only tasted of glue and paint. And when we tried to reroast the chickens at the nursery grate, they caught fire, and then they smelt of gasworks and india rubber. But I am wandering. When you remember the things that happened when you were a child,

*Mr. Noah whispered ardently, "Don't!"*

you could go on writing about them forever. I will put all this in brackets, and then you need not read it if you don't want to.)

But those painted wooden foods adhering firmly to their dishes were the kind of food of which the banquet now offered to Philip and Lucy was composed. Only they had more dishes than I had. They had as well a turkey, eight raspberry jam tarts, a pineapple, a melon, a dish of oysters in the shell, a piece of boiled bacon, and a leg of mutton. But all were equally wooden and uneatable.

Philip and Lucy, growing hungrier and hungrier, pretended with sinking hearts to eat and enjoy the wooden feast. Wine was served in those little goblets which they knew so well, where the double glasses restrained and contained a red fluid which *looked* like wine. They did not want wine, but they were thirsty as well as hungry.

Philip wondered what the waiters were. He had plenty of time to wonder while the long banquet went on. It was not till he saw a group of them standing stiffly together at the end of the hall that he knew they must be the matches with which he had once peopled a city, no other inhabitants being at hand.

When all the dishes had been handed, speeches happened.

"Friends and fellow citizens," Mr. Noah began, and went on to say how brave and clever Sir Philip was, and how likely it was that he would turn out to be the Deliverer. Philip did not hear all this speech. He was thinking of things to eat.

Then everyone in the hall stood and shouted, and Philip found that he was expected to take his turn at speech-making. He stood up trembling and wretched.

"Friends and fellow citizens," he said, "thank you very much. I want to be the Deliverer, but I don't know if I can," and sat down again amid roars of applause.

Then there was music, from a grated gallery. And then—I cannot begin to tell you how glad Lucy and Philip were—Mr. Noah said, once more in a whisper, "Cheer up! The banquet is over. *Now* we'll have tea."

"Tea" turned out to be bread and milk in a very cozy, blue silk–lined room opening out of the banqueting hall. Only Lucy, Philip, and Mr. Noah were present. Bread and milk is very good even when you have to eat it with the leaden spoons out of the dollhouse basket. When it was much later Mr. Noah suddenly said, "Good night," and in a maze of sleepy repletion (look that up in the dicker, will you?) the children went to bed. Philip's bed was of gold with yellow satin curtains, and Lucy's was made of silver, with curtains of silk that were white. But the metals and colors made no difference to their deep and dreamless sleep.

And in the morning there was bread and milk again, and the two of them had it in the blue room without Mr. Noah.

"Well," said Lucy, looking up from the bowl of white floating cubes, "do you think you're getting to like me any better?"

*"No,"* said Philip, brief and stern like the skipper in the song.

"I wish you would," said Lucy.

"Well, I can't," said Philip, "but I do want to say one thing. I'm sorry I bunked and left you. And I did come back."

"I know you did," said Lucy.

"I came back to fetch you," said Philip, "and now we'd better get along home."

"You've got to do seven deeds of power before you can get home," said Lucy.

"Oh! I remember, Perrin told me," said he.

"Well," Lucy went on, "that'll take ages. No one can go out of this place *twice* unless he's a King-Deliverer. You've gone out *once*—without *me*. Before you can go again you've got to do seven noble deeds."

"I killed the dragon," said Philip, modestly proud.

"That's only one," she said "there are six more." And she ate bread and milk with firmness.

"Do you like this adventure?" he asked abruptly.

"It's more interesting than anything that ever happened to me," she said. "If you were nice I should like it awfully. But as it is—"

"I'm sorry you don't think I'm nice," said he.

"Well, what do *you* think?" she said.

Philip reflected. He did not want not to be nice. None of us do. Though you might not think it to see how some of us behave. True politeness, he remembered having been told, consists in showing an interest in other people's affairs.

"Tell me," he said, very much wishing to be polite and nice. "Tell me what happened after I—after I—after you didn't come down the ladder with me."

"Alone and deserted," Lucy answered promptly, "my sworn friend having hooked it and left me, I fell down, and both my hands were full of gravel, and the fierce soldiery surrounded me."

"I thought you were coming just behind me," said Philip, frowning.

"Well, I wasn't."

"And then."

"Well, then—you *were* silly not to stay. They surrounded me—the soldiers, I mean—and the captain said, Tell me the truth. Are you a Destroyer or a Deliverer? So, of course, I said I wasn't a destroyer, whatever I was; and then they took me to the palace and said I could be a Princess till the Deliverer-King turned up. They said," she giggled gaily, "that my hair was the hair of a Deliverer and not of a Destroyer, and I've been most awfully happy ever since. Have you?"

"No," said Philip, remembering the miserable feeling of having been a coward and a sneak that had come upon him when he found that he had saved his own skin and left Lucy alone in an unknown and dangerous world, "not exactly happy, I shouldn't call it."

"It's beautiful being a Princess," said Lucy. "I wonder what your next noble deed will be. I wonder whether I could help you with it." She looked wistfully at him.

"If I'm going to do noble deeds I'll do them. I don't want any help, thank you, especially from girls," he answered.

"I wish you did," said Lucy, and finished her bread and milk.

Philip's bowl also was empty. He stretched arms and legs and neck.

"It is rum," he said. "Before this began I never thought a thing like this *could* begin, did you?"

"I don't know," she said, "everything's very wonderful. I've always been expecting things to be more wonderful than they ever have been. You get sort of hints and nudges, you know. Fairy tales, yes, and dreams, you can't help feeling they must mean *something*. And your sister and my daddy; the two of them being such friends when they were little, and then parted and then getting friends again—*that's* like a story in a dream, isn't it? And your building the city and me helping. And my daddy being such a dear darling and your sister being such a darling dear. It did make me think beautiful things were sort of likely. Didn't it you?"

"No," said Philip. "I mean yes," he said, and he was in that moment nearer to liking Lucy than he had ever been before, "everything's very wonderful, isn't it?"

"Ahem!" said a respectful cough behind them,

They turned to meet the calm gaze of Double-six.

"If you've quite finished breakfast, Sir Philip," he said, "Mr. Noah would be pleased to see you in his office."

"Me too?" said Lucy, before Philip could say, "Only me, I suppose?"

"You may come too, if you wish it, your highness," said Double-six, bowing stiffly.

They found Mr. Noah very busy in a little room littered with papers; he was sitting at a table writing.

"Good morning, Princess," he said, "good morning, Sir Philip. You see me very busy. I am trying to arrange for your next labor."

"Do you mean my next deed of valor?" Philip asked.

"We have decided that all your deeds need not be deeds of valor," said Mr. Noah, fiddling with a pen. "The strange labors of Hercules, you remember, were some of them dangerous and some merely difficult. I have decided that difficult things shall count. There are several things that really *need* doing," he went on half to himself. "There's the fruit supply, and the Dwellers by the sea, and—but that must wait. We try to give you as much variety as possible. Yesterday's was an out-door adventure. Today's shall be an indoor amusement. I say today's but I confess that I think it not unlikely that the task I am now about to set the candidate for the post of King-Deliverer, the task, I say, which I am now about to set you, may, quite possibly, occupy some days, if not weeks, of your valuable time."

"But our people at home," said Philip. "It isn't that I'm afraid, really and truly it isn't, but they'll go out of their minds, not knowing what's become of us. Oh, Mr. Noah! Do let us go back."

"It's all right," said Mr. Noah. "However long you stay here time won't move with them. I thought I'd explained that to you.

"But you said—"

"I said you'd set our clocks to the time of *your* world when you deserted your little friend. But when you had come back for her, and rescued her from the dragon, the clocks went their own time again. There's only just that time missing that happened between your com-ing here the second time and your killing the dragon."

"I see," said Philip. But he didn't. I only hope *you* do.

"You can take your time about this new job," said Mr. Noah, "and you may get any help you like. I shan't consider you've failed till you've been at it three months. After that the Pretenderette would be entitled to *her* chance."

"If you're quite sure that the time here doesn't count at home," said Philip, "what is it, please, that we've got to do?"

"The greatest intellects of our country have for many ages occu-pied themselves with the problem which you are now asked to solve," said Mr. Noah. "Your late jailer, Mr. Bacon-Shakespeare, has written no less than twenty-seven volumes, all in cipher, on this very subject. But as he has forgotten what cipher he used, and no one else ever knew it, his volumes are of but little use to us.

"I see," said Philip. And again he didn't.

Mr. Noah rose to his full height, and when he stood up the children looked very small beside him.

"Now," he said, "I will tell you what it is that you must do. I should like to decree that your second labor should be the tidying up of this room—*all* these papers are prophecies relating to the Deliverer—but it is one of our laws that the judge must not use any public matter for his own personal benefit. So I have decided that the next labor shall be the disentangling of the Mazy Carpet. It is in the Pillared Hall of Public Amusements. I will get my hat and we will go there at once. I can tell you about it as we go."

And as they went down streets and past houses and palaces, all of which Philip could now dimly remember to have built at some time or other. Mr. Noah went on:

"It is a very beautiful hall, but we have never been able to use it for public amusement or anything else. The giant who originally built this city placed in this hall a carpet so thick that it rises to your knees, and so intricately woven that none can disentangle it. It is far too thick to pass through any of the doors. It is your task to remove it."

"Why that's as easy as easy," said Philip. "I'll cut it in bits and bring out a bit at a time."

"That would be most unfortunate for you," said Mr. Noah. "I filed only this morning a very ancient prophecy:

> "He who shall the carpet sever,
>     By fire or flint or steel,
> Shall be fed on orange pips forever,
>     And dressed in orange peel.

You wouldn't like that, you know."

"No," said Philip grimly, "I certainly shouldn't."

"The carpet must be *unraveled,* unwoven, so that not a thread is broken. Here is the hall."

They went up steps—Philip sometimes wished he had not been so fond of building steps—and through a dark vestibule to an arched door. Looking through it they saw a great hall and at its end a raised space, more steps, and two enormous pillars of bronze wrought in relief with figures of flying birds.

"Father's Japanese vases," Lucy whispered.

The floor of the room was covered by the carpet. It was loosely but difficultly woven of very thick soft rope of a red color. When I say difficultly, I mean that it wasn't just straightforward in the weaving, but the threads went over and under and around about in such a determined and bewildering way that Philip felt—and said—that he would rather untie the string of a hundred of the most difficult parcels than tackle this.

"Well," said Mr. Noah, "I leave you to it. Board and lodging will be provided at the Provisional Palace, where you slept last night. All citizens are bound to assist when called upon. Dinner is at one. *Good* morning!"

Philip sat down in the dark archway and gazed helplessly at the twisted strands of the carpet. After a moment of hesitation Lucy sat down too, clasped her arms round her knees, and she also gazed at the carpet. They had all the appearance of shipwrecked mariners looking out over a great sea and longing for a sail.

"Ha ha—tee hee!" said a laugh close behind them. They turned. And it was the motor-veiled lady, the hateful Pretenderette, who had crept up close behind them, and was looking down at them through her veil.

"What do you want?" said Philip severely.

"I want to laugh," said the motor lady. "I want to laugh at *you*. And I'm going to."

"Well go and laugh somewhere else, then," Philip suggested.

"Ah! But this is where I want to laugh. You and your carpet! You'll never do it. You don't know how. But *I* do."

"Come away," whispered Lucy, and they went. The Pretenderette followed slowly. Outside, a couple of Dutch dolls in check suits were passing, arm in arm.

"Help!" cried Lucy suddenly, and the Dutch dolls paused and took their hats off.

"What is it?" the taller doll asked, stroking his black painted mustache.

"Mr. Noah said all citizens were bound to help us," said Lucy a little breathlessly.

"But of course," said the shorter doll, bowing with stiff courtesy.

"Then," said Lucy, "will you *please* take that motor person away and put her somewhere where she can't bother till we've done the carpet?"

"Delighted," exclaimed the agreeable Dutch strangers, darted up the steps, and next moment emerged with the form of the Pretenderette between them, struggling indeed, but struggling vainly.

"You need not have the slightest further anxiety," the taller Dutchman said. "Dismiss the incident from your mind. We will take her to the hall of justice. Her offence is bothering people in pursuit of their duty. The sentence is imprisonment for as long as the botheree chooses. Good morning."

"Oh, *thank you!*" said both the children together.

When they were alone, Philip said—and it was not easy to say it: "That was jolly clever of you, Lucy. I should never have thought of it."

"Oh, that's nothing," said Lucy, looking down. "I could do more than that."

"What?" he asked.

"I could unravel the carpet," said Lucy, with deep solemnity.

"But it's me that's got to do it," Philip urged.

"Every citizen is bound to help, if called in," Lucy reminded him. "And I suppose a princess *is* a citizen."

"Perhaps I can do it by myself," said Philip.

"Try," said Lucy, and sat down on the steps, her fairy skirts spreading out around her like a white double hollyhock.

He tried. He went back and looked at the great coarse cables of the carpet. He could see no end to the cables, no beginning to his task.

And Lucy just went on sitting there like a white hollyhock. And time went on, and presently became, rather urgently, dinnertime.

So he went back to Lucy and said:

"All right, you can show me how to do it, if you like."

But Lucy replied:

"Not much! If you want me to help you with *this*, you'll have to promise to let me help in all the other things. And you'll have to *ask* me to help—ask me politely too."

"I shan't then," said Philip. But in the end he had to—politely also.

"With pleasure," said Lucy, the moment he asked her, and he could see she had been making up what she should answer, while he was making up his mind to ask. "I shall be delighted to help you in this and all the other tasks. Say yes."

"Yes," said Philip, who was very hungry.

"In this and all the other tasks, say."

"In this and all the other tasks," he said. "Go on. How can we do it?"

"It's *crochet*," Lucy giggled. "It's a little crochet mat I'd made of red wool, and I put it in the hall that night. You've just got to find the end and pull, and it all comes undone. You just want to find the end and pull."

"It's too heavy for us to pull."

"Well," said Lucy, who had certainly had time to think everything out, "you get one of those twisty round things they pull boats out of the sea with, and I'll find the end while you're getting it."

She ran up the steps and Philip looked around the buildings on the other three sides of the square, to see if any one of them looked like a capstan shop, for he understood, as of course you also have done, that a capstan was what Lucy meant.

On a building almost opposite he read, "Naval Necessaries Supply Company," and he ran across to it.

"Rather," said the secretary of the company, a plump sailor doll, when Philip had explained his needs. "I'll send a dozen men over at once. Only too proud to help, Sir Philip. The navy is always keen on helping valor and beauty."

"I want to be brave," said Philip, "but I'd rather not be beautiful."

"Of course not," said the secretary, and added surprisingly, "I meant the Lady Lucy."

"Oh!" said Philip.

So twelve bluejackets and a capstan outside the Hall of Public Amusements were soon the center of a cheering crowd. Lucy had found the end of the rope, and two sailors dragged it out and attached it to the capstan, and then—round and round with a will and a breathless chanty—the carpet was swiftly unraveled. Dozens of eager helpers stood on the parts of the carpet which were not being unraveled, to keep it steady while the pulling went on.

The news of Philip's success spread like wildfire through the city, and the crowds gathered thicker and thicker. The great doors beyond the pillars with the birds on them were thrown open, and Mr. Noah and the principal citizens stood there to see the end of the unraveling.

"Bravo!" said everyone in tremendous enthusiasm. "Bravo! Sir Philip."

"It wasn't me," said Philip difficultly, when the crowd paused for breath, "it was Lucy thought of it."

"Bravo! Bravo!" shouted the crowd louder than ever. "Bravo, for the Lady Lucy! Bravo for Sir Philip, the modest truth-teller!"

"Bravo, my dear," said Mr. Noah, waving his hat and thumping Lucy on the back.

"I'm awfully glad I thought of it," she said. "That makes two deeds Sir Philip's done, doesn't it? Two out of the seven."

"Yes, indeed," said Mr. Noah enthusiastically. "I must make him a Baronet now. His title will grow grander with each deed. There's an old prophecy that the person who finds out how to unravel the carpet must be the first to dance in the Hall of Public Amusements.

*So, all down the wide clear floor . . . Lucy danced.*

"The clever one, the noble one,
Who makes the carpet come undone,
Shall be the first to dance a measure
Within the Hall of Public Pleasure.

"I suppose public *amusement* was too difficult a rhyme even for these highly skilled poets, our astrologers. You, my child, seem to have been well inspired in your choice of a costume. Dance, then, my Lady Lucy, and let the prophecy be fulfilled."

So, all down the wide clear floor of the Hall of Public Amusement, Lucy danced. And the people of the city looked on and applauded. Philip with the rest.

# CHAPTER SIX

# The Lions in the Desert

"BUT WHY?" asked Philip at dinner, which was no painted wonder of wooden make-believe, but real roast guinea fowl and angel pudding. "Why do you only have wooden things to eat at your banquets?"

"Banquets are extremely important occasions," said Mr. Noah, "and real food—food that you can eat and enjoy—only serves to distract the mind from the serious affairs of life. Many of the most successful caterers in your world have grasped this great truth."

"But why," Lucy asked, "do you have the big silver bowls with nothing in them?"

Mr. Noah sighed. "The bowls are for dessert," he said.

"But there isn't any dessert *in* them," Lucy objected.

"No," said Mr. Noah, sighing again, "that's just it. There is no dessert. There has never been any dessert. Will you have a little more angel pudding?"

It was quite plain to Lucy and Philip that Mr. Noah wished to change the subject, which, for some reason, was a sad one, and with true politeness they both said, "Yes, please," to the angel pudding offer, though they had already had quite as much as they really needed.

After dinner Mr. Noah took them for a walk through the town, "to see the factories," he said. This surprised Philip, who had been taught not to build factories with his bricks because factories were so ugly, but the factories turned out to be pleasant, long, low houses, with tall French windows opening into gardens of roses, where people of all nations made beautiful and useful things, and loved making them. And all the people who were making them looked clean and happy.

"I wish we had factories like those," Philip said. "Our factories *are* so ugly. Helen says so."

"That's because all your factories are *money* factories," said Mr. Noah, "though they're called by all sorts of different names. Everyone here has to make something that isn't just money or *for* money—something useful *and* beautiful."

"Even you?" said Lucy.

"Even I," said Mr. Noah.

"What do you make?" The question was bound to come.

"Laws, of course," Mr. Noah answered in some surprise. "Didn't you know I was the Chief Judge?"

"But laws can't be useful and beautiful, can they?"

"They can certainly be useful," said Mr. Noah, "and," he added with modest pride, "my laws are beautiful. What do you think of this? 'Everybody must try to be kind to everybody else. Anyone who has been unkind must be sorry and say so.'"

"It seems all right," said Philip, "but it's not exactly beautiful."

"Oh, don't you think so?" said Mr. Noah, a little hurt. "It mayn't *sound* beautiful perhaps—I never could write poetry—but it's quite beautiful when people do it."

"Oh, if you mean your laws are beautiful when they're *kept*," said Philip.

"Beautiful things can't be beautiful when they're broken, of course," Mr. Noah explained. "Not even laws. But ugly laws are only beautiful when they *are* broken. That's odd, isn't it? Laws are very tricky things."

"I say," Philip said suddenly, as they climbed one of the steep flights of steps between trees in pots, "couldn't we do another of the deeds now? I don't feel as if I'd really done anything today at all. It was Lucy who did the carpet. Do tell us the next deed."

"The next deed," Mr. Noah answered, "will probably take some time. There's no reason why you should not begin it today if you like. It is a deed peculiarly suited to a baronet. I don't know why," he added hastily, "it may be that it is the only thing that baronets are good for. I shouldn't wonder. The existence of baronets," he added musingly, "has always seemed to the thoughtful to lack justification. Perhaps this deed which you will begin today is the wise end to which baronets were designed."

"Yes, I daresay," said Philip "but what is the end?"

"I don't know," Mr. Noah owned, "but I'll tell you what the *deed* is. You've got to journey to the land of the Dwellers by the Sea and, by any means that may commend itself to you, slay their fear."

Philip naturally asked what the Dwellers by the Sea were afraid of.

"That you will learn from them," said Mr. Noah, "but it is a very great fear."

"Is it something we shall be afraid of *too*?" Lucy asked. And Philip at once said, "Oh, then she really did mean to come, did she? But she wasn't to if she was afraid. Girls weren't expected to be brave."

"They *are*, here," said Mr. Noah, "the girls are expected to be brave and the boys kind."

"Oh," said Philip doubtfully. And Lucy said:

"Of course I meant to come. You know you promised."

So that was settled.

"And now," said Mr. Noah, rubbing his hands with the cheerful air of one who has a great deal to do and is going to enjoy doing it, "we must fit you out a proper expedition, for the Dwellers by the Sea are a very long way off. What would you like to ride on?"

"A horse," said Philip, truly pleased. He said horse, because he did not want to ride a donkey, and he had never seen anyone ride any animal but these two.

"That's right," Mr. Noah said, patting him on the back. "I *was* so afraid you'd ask for a bicycle. And there's a dreadful law here—it was made by mistake, but there it is—that if anyone asks for machinery they have to have it and keep on using it. But as to a horse. Well, I'm not sure. You see, you have to ride right across the pebbly waste, and it's a good three days' journey. But come along to the stables."

You know the kind of stables they would be? The long shed with stalls such as you had, when you were little, for your little wooden horses and carts? Only there were not only horses here, but every sort of animal that has ever been ridden on. Elephants, camels, donkeys, mules, bulls, goats, zebras, tortoises, ostriches, bisons, and pigs. And in the last stall of all, which was not of common wood but of beaten silver, stood the very Hippogriff himself, with his long white mane and his long white tail, and his gentle beautiful eyes. His long white wings were folded neatly on his satin-smooth back, and how he and the stall got here was more than Philip could guess. All the others were Noah's Ark animals, alive, of course, but still Noah's Arky beyond possibility of mistake. But the Hippogriff was not Noah's Ark at all.

"He came," Mr. Noah explained, "out of a book. One of the books you used to build your city with."

"Can't we have *him?*" Lucy said. "He looks such a darling." And the Hippogriff turned his white velvet nose and nuzzled against her in affectionate acknowledgment of the compliment.

"Not if you both go," Mr. Noah explained. "He cannot carry more than one person at a time unless one is an Earl. No, if I may advise, I should say go by camel."

"Can the camel carry two?"

"Of course. He is called the ship of the desert," Mr. Noah informed them, "and a ship that wouldn't carry more than one would be simply silly."

So *that* was settled. Mr. Noah himself saddled and bridled the camel, which was a very large one, with his own hands.

"Let me see," he said, standing thoughtful with the lead rope in his hand, "you'll be wanting dogs—"

"I *always* want dogs," said Philip warmly.

"—to use in emergencies." He whistled and two Noah's Ark dogs leaped from their kennels to their chains' end. They were dachshunds, very long and low, and very alike except that one was a little bigger and a little browner than the other.

"This is your master and that's your mistress," Mr. Noah explained to the dogs, and they fawned around the children.

"Then you'll want things to eat and things to drink and tents and umbrellas in case of bad weather, and—but let's turn down this street; just at the corner we shall find exactly what we want."

It was a shop that said outside "Universal Provider. Expeditions fitted out at a moment's notice. Punctuality and dispatch." The shopkeeper came forward politely. He was so exactly like Mr. Noah that the children knew who he was even before he said, "Well, Father," and Mr. Noah said, "This is my son: he has had some experience in outfits."

"What have you got to start with?" the son asked, getting to business at once.

"Two dogs, two children, and a camel," said Mr. Noah. "Yes, I know it's customary to have two of everything, but I assure you, my dear boy, that one camel is as much as Sir Philip can manage. It is indeed."

Mr. Noah's son very dutifully supposed that his father knew best and willingly agreed to provide everything that was needed for the expedition, including one best-quality talking parrot, and to deliver all goods, carefully packed, within half an hour.

So now you see Philip, and Lucy, who still wore her fairy dress, packed with all their belongings on the top of a very large and wobbly camel,

*On the top of a very large and wobbly camel*

and being led out of the city by the usual procession, with seven bands of music all playing "See the Conquering Hero Goes," quite a different tune from the one you know, which has a name a little like that.

The camel and its load were rather a tight fit for the particular gateway that they happened to go out by, and the children had to stoop to avoid scraping their heads against the top of the arch. But they got through all right, and now they were well on the road, which was really little more than a field path running through the flowery meadow country where the dragon had been killed. They saw the Stonehenge ruins and the big tower far away to the left, and in front lay the vast and interesting expanse of the Absolutely Unknown.

The sun was shining—there was a sun, and Mr. Noah had told the children that it came out of the poetry books, together with rain and flowers and the changing seasons—and in spite of the strange, almost-tumble-no-it's-all-right-but-you'd-better-look-out way in which the camel walked, the two travelers were very happy. The dogs bounded along in the best of spirits, and even the camel seemed less a prey than usual to that proud melancholy which you must have noticed in your visits to the zoo as his most striking quality.

It was certainly very grand to ride on a camel, and Lucy tried not to think how difficult it would be to get on and off. The parrot was interesting too. It talked extremely well. Of course, you understand that if you can only make a parrot understand, it can tell you everything you want to know about other animals, because it understands *their* talk quite naturally and without being made. The present parrot declined ordinary conversation, and when questioned only recited poetry of a rather dull kind that went on and on. "Arms and the man I sing" it began, and then something about haughty Juno. Its voice was soothing, and riding on the camel was not unlike being rocked in a very bumpety cradle. The children were securely seated in things like padded panniers, and they had had an exciting day. As the sun set, which it did quite soon, the parrot called out to the nearest dog, "I say, Max, they're asleep."

"I don't wonder," said Max. "But it's all right. Humpty knows the way."

"Keep a civil tongue in your head, you young dog, can't you?" said the camel grumpily.

"Don't be cross, darling," said the other dog, whose name was Brenda, "and be sure you stop at a really first-class oasis for the night. But I know we can trust *you*, dear."

The camel muttered that it was all very well, but his voice was not quite as cross as before.

After that the expedition went on in silence through the deepening twilight.

A tumbling, shaking, dumping sensation, more like a soft railway accident than anything else, awakened our travelers, and they found that the camel was kneeling down.

"Off you come," said the parrot, "and make the fire and boil the kettle."

"Polly put the kettle on," Lucy said absently, as she slid down to the ground, to which the parrot replied, "Certainly not. I wish you wouldn't rake up that old story. It was quite false. I never did put a kettle on, and I never will."

Why should I describe to you the adventure of camping at an oasis in a desert? You must all have done it many times; or if you have not done it, you have read about it. You know all about the well and the palm trees and the dates and things. They had cocoa for supper. It was great fun, and they slept soundly and awoke in the morning with a heart for any fate, as a respectable poet puts it.

The next day was just the same as the first, only instead of going through fresh green fields, the way lay through dry yellow desert. And again the children slept, and again the camel chose an oasis with remarkable taste and judgment. But the second night was not at all the same as the first. For in the middle of it the parrot awakened Philip by biting his ear, and then hopping to a safe distance from his awakening fists and crying out, "Make up the campfire—look alive. It's lions."

The dogs were whining and barking, and Brenda was earnestly trying to climb a palm tree. Max faced the danger, it is true, but he seemed to have no real love of sport.

Philip sprang up and heaped dead palm scales and leaves on the dying fire. It blazed up and something moved beyond the bushes. Philip wondered whether those pairs of shining things, like strayed stars, that he saw in the darkness could really be the eyes of lions.

"What a nuisance these lions are, to be sure," said the parrot. "No, they won't come near us while the fire's burning, but really, they ought to be put down by law."

"Why doesn't somebody kill them?" Lucy asked. She had wakened when Philip did, and, after a meditative minute, had helped with the palm scales and things.

"It's not so easy," said the parrot, "nobody knows how to do it. How would *you* kill a lion?"

"*I* don't know," said Philip, but Lucy said, "are they Noah's Ark lions?"

"Of course they are," said Polly, "all the books with lions in them are kept shut up."

"I know how you could kill Noah's Ark lions if you could catch them," Lucy said.

"It's easy enough to catch them," said Polly. "An hour after dawn they go to sleep, but it's unsportsmanlike to kill game when it's asleep."

"I'm going to think, if you don't mind," Lucy announced, and sat down very near the fire. "It's just the opposite of the dragon," she said after a minute. The parrot nodded and there was a long silence. Then suddenly Lucy jumped up.

"I know," she cried, "oh—I really *do* know. And it won't hurt them either. I don't a bit mind killing things, but I do hate hurting them. There's plenty of rope, I know."

There was.

"Then when it's dawn we'll tie them up and then you'll see."

"I think you might tell *me*," said Philip, injured.

"No—they may understand what we say. Polly does."

Philip made a natural suggestion. But Lucy replied that it was not manners to whisper, and the parrot said that it should think not indeed.

So, sitting by the fire, all faces turned to where those strange twin stars shone and those strange hidden movements and rustlings stirred, the expedition waited for the dawn. Brenda had given up the tree-climbing idea, and was cuddling up as close to Lucy as possible. The camel, who had been trembling with fear all the while, tried to cuddle up to Philip, which would have been easier if it had been a smaller kind instead of being, as it was, what Mr. Noah's son, the Universal Provider, had called, "an out size in camels."

And presently dawn came, not slow and silvery as dawns come here, but sudden and red, with strong level lights and the shadows of the palm trees stretching all across the desert.

In broad daylight it did not seem so hard to have to go and look for the lions. They all went—even the camel pulled himself together to join the lion hunt, and Brenda herself decided to come rather than be left alone.

The lions were easily found. There were only two of them, of course, and they were lying close together, each on its tawny side on the sandy desert at the edge of the oasis.

Very gently the ropes, with slipknots, were fitted over their heads, and the other end of the rope passed around a palm tree. Other ropes around the trees were passed around what would have been the waists of the lions if lions had such things as waists.

"Now!" whispered Lucy, and at once all four ropes were pulled tight. The lions struggled, but only in their sleep. And soon they were still. Then with more and more ropes their legs and tails were made fast.

"And that's all right," said Lucy, rather out of breath. "Where's Polly?"

"Here," replied that bird from a neighboring bush. "I thought I should only be in the way if I kept close to you. But I longed to lend a claw in such good work. Can I help *now*?"

"Will you please explain to the dogs?" said Lucy. "It's their turn now. The only way I know to kill Noah's Ark lions is to *lick the paint off* and break their legs. And if the dogs lick all the paint off their legs they won't feel it when we break them."

Polly hastened to explain to the dogs, and then turned again to Lucy.

"They asked if you're sure the ropes will hold, and I've told them of course. So now they're going to begin. I only hope the paint won't make them ill."

"It never did me," said Lucy. "I sucked the dove quite clean one Sunday, and it wasn't half bad. Tasted of sugar a little and eucalyptus oil like they give you when you've got a cold. Tell them that, Polly."

Polly did, and added, "I will recite poetry to them to hearten them to their task."

"Do," said Philip heartily, "it may make them hurry up. But perhaps you'd better tell them that we shall pinch their tails if they happen to go to sleep."

Then the children had a cocoa-and-date breakfast. (All expeditions seem to live mostly on cocoa, and when they come back they often write to the cocoa makers to say how good it was and they don't know what they would have done without it.) And the noble and devoted dogs licked and licked and licked, and the paint began to come off the lions' legs like anything. It was heavy work turning the lions over so as to get at the other or unlicked side, but the expedition worked with a will, and the lions resisted but feebly, being still asleep, and, besides, weak from loss of paint. And the dogs had a drink given them and were patted and praised, and set to work again. And they licked and licked for hours and hours. And in the end all the paint was off the lions' legs, and Philip chopped them off with the explorer's axe, which that experienced Provider, Mr. Noah's son, had thoughtfully

*It was heavy work turning the lions over.*

included in the outfit of the expedition. And as he chopped the chips flew, and Lucy picked one up, and it was *wood*, just wood and nothing else, though when they had tied it up it had been real writhing resisting lion leg and no mistake. And when all the legs were chopped off, Philip put his hand on a lion body, and that was wood too. So the lions were dead indeed.

"It seems a pity," he said. "Lions are such jolly beasts when they are alive."

"I never cared for lions myself," said Polly; and Lucy said, "Never mind, Phil. It didn't hurt them, anyway."

And that was the first time she ever called him Phil.

"All right, Lu," said Philip. "It was jolly clever of you to think of it anyhow."

And that was the first time he ever called her Lu.

They saw the straight pale line of the sea for a long time before they came to the place of the Dwellers by the Sea. For these people had built their castle down on the very edge of the sea, and the Pebbly Waste rose and rose to a mountain that hid their castle from the eyes of the camel riders who were now drawing near to the scene of their next deed. The Pebbly Waste was all made of small slippery stones, and the children understood how horrid a horse would have found it. Even the camel went very slowly, and the dogs no longer frisked and bounded, but went at a foot's pace with drooping ears and tails.

"I should call a halt, if I were you," said Polly. "We shall all be the better for a cup of cocoa. And besides—"

Polly refused to explain this dark hint and only added, "Look out for surprises."

"I thought," said Philip, draining the last of his second mug of cocoa, "I thought there were no birds in the desert except you, and you're more a person than a bird. But look there."

Far away across the desert a moving speck showed, high up in the blue air. It grew bigger and bigger, plainly coming toward the camp.

It was as big as a moth now, now as big as a teacup, now as big as an eagle, and—

"But it's got four legs," said Lucy.

"Yes," said the parrot, "it would have, you know. It is the Hippogriff."

It was indeed that magnificent wonder. Flying through the air with long sweeps of his great white wings, the Hippogriff drew nearer and nearer, bearing on his back—what?

"It's the Pretenderette," cried Lucy, and at the same moment Philip said, "It's that nasty motor thing."

It was. The Hippogriff dropped from the sky to the desert below as softly as a butterfly alighting on a flower, and stood there in all his gracious whiteness. And on his back was the veiled motor lady.

"So glad I've caught you up," she said in that hateful voice of hers. "Now we can go on together."

"I don't see what you wanted to come at all for," said Philip downrightly.

"Oh, *don't* you?" she said, sitting up there on the Hippogriff with her horrid motor veil fluttering in the breeze from the now hidden sea. "Why, of course, I have a right to be present at all experiments. There ought to be some responsible grown-up person to see that you really do what you're sure to say you've done."

"Do you mean that we're liars?" Philip asked hotly.

"I don't mean to *say* anything about it," the Pretenderette answered with an unpleasant giggle, "but a grown-up person ought to be present." She added something about a parcel of birds and children. And the parrot ruffled his feathers till he looked twice his proper size.

Philip said he didn't see it.

"Oh, but *I* do," said the Pretenderette. "If you fail, then it's my turn, and I might very likely succeed the minute after you'd failed. So we'll all go on comfortably together. *Won't* that be nice?"

A speechless despair seemed to have fallen on the party. Nobody spoke. The children looked blank, the dogs whined, the camel put on his haughtiest sneer, and the parrot fidgeted in his fluffed-out feather dress.

"Let's be starting," said the motor lady. "Gee-up, pony!" A shiver ran through everyone present. That a Pretenderette should dare to speak so to a Hippogriff!

Suddenly the parrot spread its wings and flew to perch on Philip's shoulder. It whispered in his ear.

"Whispering is not manners, I know," it said, "but your own generous heart will excuse me. 'Parcel of birds and children.' Doesn't your blood boil?"

Philip thought it did.

"Well, then," said the bird impatiently, "what are we waiting for? You've only got to say the word and I'll take her back by the ear."

"I wish you would," said Philip from the heart.

"Nothing easier," said the parrot, "the miserable outsider! Intruding into *our* expedition! I advise you to await my return here. Or if I am not back by the morning there will be no objection to your calling, about noon, on the Dwellers. I can rejoin you there. Good-bye."

It stroked his ear with a gentle and kindly beak and flew into the air and circled three times round the detested motor lady's head.

"Get away," she cried, flapping her hands furiously. "Call your silly Poll-parrot off, can't you?" And then she screamed, "Oh! it's got hold of my ear!"

"Oh, don't hurt her," said Lucy.

"I will not hurt her." The parrot let the ear go on purpose to say this, and the Pretenderette covered both ears with her hands. "You person in the veil, I shall take hold again in a moment. And it will hurt you much less if the Hippogriff and I happen to be flying in the same direction. See? If I were you I should just say, 'Go back the way you came, please,' to the Hippogriff, and then I shall hardly hurt you at all. Don't think of getting off. If you do, the dogs will have you. Keep your hands over your ears if you like. I know you can hear me well enough. Now I am going to take hold of you again. Keep your hands where they are. I'm not particular to an ear or so. A nose will do just as well."

The person on the Hippogriff put both hands to her nose. Instantly the parrot had her again by the ear.

"Go back the way you came," she cried, "but I'll be even with you children yet."

The Hippogriff did not move.

"Let go my ear," screamed the lady.

"You'll have to say please, you know," said Philip. "Not to the bird, I don't mean that: that's no good. But to the Hippogriff."

"*Please* then," said the lady in a burst of temper, and instantly the white wings parted and spread and the Hippogriff rose in the air. Polly let the ear go for the moment to say:

"I shan't hurt her so long as she behaves," and then took hold again and his little gray wings and the big white wings of the Hippogriff went sailing away across the desert.

"What a treasure of a parrot," said Philip. But Lucy said:

"Who *is* that Pretenderette? Why is she so horrid to us when everyone else is so nice?"

"I don't know," said Philip, "hateful old thing."

"I can't help feeling as if I knew her quite well, if I could only remember who she is."

"Do you?" said Philip. "I say, let's play noughts and crosses. I've got a notebook and a bit of pencil in my pocket. We might play till it's time to go to sleep."

So they played noughts and crosses on the Pebbly Waste, and behind them the parrot and the Hippogriff took away the tiresome one, and in front of them lay the high pebble ridge that was like a mountain, and beyond that was the unknown and the adventure and the Dwellers and the deed to be done.

## CHAPTER SEVEN
# The Dwellers by the Sea

YOU SOON get used to things. It seemed quite natural and home-like to Philip to be wakened in bright early out-of-doors morning by the gentle beak of the parrot at his ear.

"You got back all right, then," he said sleepily.

"It was rather a long journey," said the parrot, "but I thought it better to come back by wing. The Hippogriff offered to bring me; he is the soul of courteous gentleness. But he was tired too. The Pretenderette is in jail for the moment, but I'm afraid she'll get out again; we're so unused to having prisoners, you see. And it's no use putting *her* on her honor, because—"

"Because she hasn't any," Philip finished.

"I wouldn't say *that*," said the parrot, "of anybody. I'd only say we haven't come across it. What about breakfast?"

"How meals do keep happening," said Lucy, yawning. "It seems only a few minutes since supper. And yet here we are, hungry again."

"Ah!" said the parrot. "That's what people always feel when they have to get their meals themselves!"

When the camel and the dogs had been served with breakfast, the children and the parrot sat down to eat. And there were many questions to ask. The parrot answered some, and some it didn't answer.

"But there's one thing," said Lucy, "I do most awfully want to know. About the Hippogriff. How did it get out of the book?"

"It's a long story," said the parrot, "so I'll tell it shortly. That's a very good rule. Tell short stories longly and long stories shortly. Many years ago, in repairing one of the buildings, the masons removed the supports of one of the books which are part of the architecture. The book fell. It fell open, and out came the Hippogriff. Then they saw something struggling under the next page and lifted it, and out came a megatherium. So they shut the book and built it into the wall again."

"But how did the megawhatsitsname and the Hippogriff come to be the proper size?"

"Ah that's one of the eleven mysteries. Some sages suppose that the country gave itself a sort of shake and everything settled down into the size it ought to be. I think myself that it's the air. The moment you breathe this enchanted air you become the right size. *You* did, you know."

"But why did they shut the book?"

"It was a book of beasts. Who knows what might have come out next? A tiger perhaps. And ravening for its prey as likely as not."

"I see," said Philip. "And of course beasts weren't really *needed*, because of there being all the Noah's Ark ones."

"Yes," said the parrot, "so they shut the book."

"But the weather came out of books?"

"That was another book, a poetry book. It had only one cover, so everything that was on the last page got out naturally. We got a lot out of that page, rain and sun and sky and clouds, mountains, gardens, roses, lilies, flowers in general, 'blossoms of delight' they were called in the book, and trees and the sea, and the desert and silver and iron— as much of all of them as anybody could possibly want. There are no limits to poets' imaginations, you know."

"I see," said Lucy, and took a large bite of cake. "And where did you come from, Polly, dear?"

"I," said the parrot modestly, "came out of the same book as the Hippogriff. We were on the same page. My wings entitled me to associate with him, of course, but I have sometimes thought they just put me in as a contrast. My smallness, his greatness; my red and green, his white."

"I see," said Lucy again, "and please will you tell us—"

"Enough of this," said the parrot. "Business before pleasure. You have begun the day with the pleasures of my conversation. You will have to work very hard to pay for this privilege."

So they washed up the breakfast things in warm water obligingly provided by the camel.

"And now," said the parrot, "we must pack up and go on our way to destroy the fear of the Dwellers by the Sea."

"I wonder," Brenda said to Max in an undertone, "I wonder whether it wouldn't be best for dear little dogs to lose themselves? We could turn up later, and be so *very* glad to be found."

"But why?" Max asked.

"I've noticed," said Brenda, sidling up to him with eager affectionateness, "that wherever there's fear there's something to be afraid of, even if it's only your fancy. It would be dreadful for dear little dogs to be afraid, Max, wouldn't it? So undignified."

"My dear," said Max heavily, "I could give seven noble reasons for being faithful to our master. But I will only give you one. There is nothing to eat in the desert, and nothing to drink."

"You always were so noble, dearest," said Brenda, "so different from poor little me. I've only my affectionate nature. I know I'm only a silly little thing."

So when the camel lurched forward and the parrot took wing, the dogs followed closely.

"Dear faithful things," said Lucy. "Brenda! Max! Nice dogs!"

And the dogs, politely responding, bounded enthusiastically.

The journey was not long. Quite soon they found a sort of ravine or gully in the cliff, and a path that led through it. And then they were on the beach, very pebbly with small stones, and there was the home of the Dwellers by the Sea; and beyond it, broad and blue and beautiful, the sea by which they dwelled.

The Dwelling seemed to be a sort of town of rounded buildings more like lime-kilns than anything else, with arched doors leading to dark insides. They were all built of tiny stones, such as lay on the beach. Beyond the huts or houses towered the castle, a vast rough structure with towers and arches and buttresses and bastions and glacis and bridges and a great moat all around it.

"But I never built a city like that, did you?" Lucy asked as they drew near.

"No," Philip answered. "At least—do you know, I do believe it's the sand castle Helen and I built last summer at Dymchurch. And those huts are the molds I made of my pail—with the edges worn off, you know."

Toward the castle the travelers advanced, the camel lurching like a boat on a rough sea, and the dogs going with catlike delicacy over the stones. They skirted large pools and tall seaweed-covered rocks. Along a road broad enough for twelve chariots to have driven on it abreast, slowly they came to the great gate of the castle. And as they got nearer, they saw at every window heads leaning out; every battlement, every terrace, was crowded with figures. And when they were quite near, by throwing their heads very far back, so that their necks felt quite stiff for quite a long time afterward, the children could see that all those people seemed quite young, and seemed to have very odd and delightful clothes—just a garment from shoulder to knee made, as it seemed, of dark fur.

"What lots of them there are," said Philip. "Where did they come from?"

"Out of a book," said the parrot, "but the authorities were very prompt that time. Only a line and a half got out.

*Slowly they came to the great gate of the castle.*

"Happy troops
Of gentle islanders.

Those are the islanders."

"Then why," asked Philip naturally, "aren't they on an island?"

"There's only one island, and no one is allowed on that except two people who never go there. But the islanders are happy even if they don't live on an island—always happy, except for the great fear."

Here the travelers began to cross one of the bridges across the moat, the bridge, in fact, that led to the biggest arch of all. It was a very rough arch, like the entrance to a cave.

And from out its dark mouth came a little crowd of people. "They're savages," said Lucy, shrinking till she seemed only an extra hump on the camel's back.

They were indeed of a dark complexion, sunburned in fact, but their faces were handsome and kindly. They waved friendly hands and smiled in the most agreeable and welcoming way.

The tallest islander stepped out from the crowd. He was about as big as Philip.

"They're not savages," said Philip, "don't be a donkey. They're just children."

"Hush!" said the parrot. "The Lord High Islander is now about to begin the state address of welcome!"

He was. And this was the address.

"How jolly of you to come. Do get down off that camel and come indoors and have some grub. Jim, you might take that camel around to the stable and rub him down a bit. You'd like to keep the dogs with you, of course. And what about the parrot?"

"Thanks awfully," Philip responded, and slid off the camel, followed by Lucy. "The parrot will make his own mind up—he always does."

They all trooped into the hall of the castle, which was more like a cave than a hall and very dark, for the windows were little and high

121

up. As Lucy's eyes got used to the light she perceived that the clothes of the islanders were not of skins but of seaweed.

"I asked you in," said the Lord High Islander, a jolly-looking boy of about Philip's age, "out of politeness. But really it isn't dinnertime, and the meet is in half an hour. So, unless you're really hungry—?"

The children said, "Not at all!"

"You hunt, of course?" the Lord High Islander said. "It's really the only sport we get here, except fishing. Of course, we play games and all that. I do hope you won't be dull."

"We came here on business," the parrot remarked—and the happy islanders crowded around to see him, remarking—"these are Philip and Lucy, claimants to the Deliverership. They are doing their deeds, you know," the parrot ended.

Lucy whispered, "It's really *Philip* who is the claimant, not me, only the parrot's so polite."

The Lord High Islander frowned. "We can talk about that afterward," he said, "it's a pity to waste time now."

"What do you hunt?" Philip asked.

"All the different kinds of graibeeste and the vertoblancs, and the blugraiwee, when we can find him," said the Lord High Islander. "But he's very scarce. Pinkuggers are more common, and much bigger, of course. Well, you'll soon see. If your camel's not quite fresh I can mount you both. What kind of animal do you prefer?"

"What do you ride?" Philip asked.

It appeared that the Lord High Islander rode a giraffe, and Philip longed to ride another. But Lucy said she would rather ride what she was used to, thank you.

When they got out into the courtyard of the castle, they found it full of a crowd of animals, any of which you may find in the zoo, or in your old Noah's ark if it was a sufficiently expensive one to begin with, and if you have not broken or lost too many of the inhabitants. Each animal had its rider and the party rode out onto the beach.

*"If your camel's not quite fresh I can mount you both."*

"What *is* it they hunt?" Philip asked the parrot, who had perched on his shoulder.

"All the little animals in the Noah's ark that haven't any names," the parrot told him. "All those are considered fair game. Hullo! Blugraiwee!" it shouted, as a little gray beast with blue spots started from the shelter of a rock and made for the cover of a patch of giant seaweed. Then all sorts of little animals got up and scurried off into places of security.

"There goes a vertoblanc," said the parrot, pointing to a bright green animal of uncertain shape, whose breast and paws were white, "and there's a graibeeste."

The graibeeste was about as big as a fox, and had rabbit's ears and the unusual distinction of a tail coming out of his back just halfway between one end of him and the other. But there are graibeestes of all sorts and shapes.

You know when people are making the animals for Noah's arks they make the big ones first, elephants and lions and tigers and so on, and paint them as nearly as they can the right colors. Then they get weary of copying nature and begin to paint the animals pink and green and chocolate color, which in nature is not the case. These are the chockmunks, and vertoblancs and the pinkuggers. And presently the makers get sick of the whole business and make the animals any sort of shape and paint them all one gray—these are the graibeestes. And at the very end a guilty feeling of having been slackers comes over the makers of the Noah's arks, and they paint blue spots on the last and littlest of the graibeestes to ease their consciences. This is the blugraiwee.

"Tally Ho! Hark forrad! Yoicks!" were some of the observations now to be heard on every side as the hunt swept on, the blugraiwee well ahead. Dogs yapped, animals galloped, riders shouted, the sun shone, the sea sparkled, and far ahead the blugraiwee ran, extended to his full length like a gray straight line. He was killed five miles from the castle after a splendid run. And when a pinkugger had been secured and half a dozen graibeeste, the hunt rode slowly home.

"We only hunt to kill and we only kill for food," the Lord High Islander said.

"But," said Philip, "I thought Noah's ark animals turned into wood when they were dead."

"Not if you kill for food. The intention makes all the difference. I had a plum-cake intention when we put up the blugraiwee, the pinkugger I made a bread-and-butter intention about, and the graibeestes I intended for rice pudding and prunes and toffee and ices and all sorts of odd things. So, of course, when we come to cut them up they'll *be* what I intended."

"I see," said Philip, jogging along on his camel. "I say," he added, "you don't mind my asking—how is it you're all children here?"

"Well," said the Lord High Islander, "it's ancient history, so I don't suppose it's true. But they say that when the government had to make sure that we should always be *happy* troops of gentle islanders, they decided that the only way was for us to be children. And we do have the most ripping time. And we do our own hunting and cooking and wash up our own plates and things, and for heavy work we have the M.A.'s. They're men who've had to work at sums and history and things at college so hard that they want a holiday. So they come here and work for us, and if any of us do want to learn anything, the M.A.'s are handy to have about the place. It pleases them to teach anything, poor things. They live in the huts. There's always a long list waiting for their turn. Oh yes, they wear the seaweed dress the same as we do. And they hunt on Tuesdays, Thursdays, and Saturdays. They hunt big game, the fierce ambergris who is gray with a yellow stomach and the bigger graibeestes. Now, we'll have dinner the minute we get in, and then we must talk about It."

The game was skinned and cut up in the courtyard, and the intentions of the Lord High Islander had certainly been carried out. For the blugraiwee was plum cake, and the other animals just what was needed.

And after dinner the Lord High Islander took Lucy and Philip up onto the top of the highest tower, and the three lay in the sun eating toffee and gazing out over the sea at the faint distant blue of the island.

"The island where we aren't allowed to go," as the Lord High Islander sadly pointed out.

"Now," said Lucy gently, "you won't mind telling us what you're afraid of? Don't mind telling us. *We're* afraid too; we're afraid of all sorts of things quite often."

"Speak for yourself," said Philip, but not unkindly. "I'm not so jolly often afraid as you seem to think. Go ahead, my Lord."

"You might as well call me Billy," said the Lord High Islander, "it's my name."

"Well, Billy, then. What is it you're afraid of?"

"I hate being afraid," said Billy angrily. "Of course, I know no true boy is afraid of anything except doing wrong. One of the M.A.'s told me that. But the M.A.'s are afraid too."

"What of?" Lucy asked, glancing at the terrace below, where already the shadows were lengthening. "It'll be getting dark soon. I'd much rather know what you're afraid of while it's daylight."

"What we're afraid of," said Billy abruptly, "is the sea. Suppose a great wave came and washed away the castle, and the huts, and the MA's, and all of us?"

"But it never *has*, has it?" Lucy asked.

"No, but everything must have a beginning. I know that's true, because another of the M.A.'s told it me."

"But why don't you go and live somewhere inland?"

"Because we couldn't live away from the sea. We're islanders, you know; we couldn't bear not to be near the sea. And we'd rather be afraid of it, than not have it to be afraid of. But it upsets the government, because we ought to be *happy* troops of gentle islanders, and you can't be quite happy if you're afraid. That's why it's one of your deeds to take away our fear."

"It sounds jolly difficult," said Philip. "I shall have to think," he added desperately. So he lay and thought with Max and Brenda asleep by his side and the parrot preening its bright feathers on the parapet of the tower, while Lucy and the Lord High Islander played cat's cradle with a long thread of seaweed.

"It's supper time," said Billy at last. "Have you thought of anything?"

"Not a single thing," said Philip.

"Well, don't swat over it anymore," said Billy. "Just stay with us and have a jolly time. You're sure to think of something. Or else Lucy will. We'll act charades tonight."

They did. The rest of the islanders were an extremely jolly lot, and all the M.A.'s came out of their huts to be audience. It was a charming evening, and ended up with hide-and-seek all over the castle.

To wake next morning on a bed of soft, dry, sweet-smelling seaweed, and to know that the day was to be spent in having a good time with the jolliest set of children she had ever met, was delightful to Lucy. Philip's delight was dashed by the knowledge that he must, sooner or later, *think*. But the day passed most agreeably. They all bathed in the rock pools, picked up shellfish for dinner, played rounders in the afternoon, and in the evening danced to the music made by the M.A.'s, who most of them carried flutes in their pockets, and who were all very flattered at being asked to play.

So the pleasant days went on. Every morning Philip said to himself, "Now, today I really *must* think of something," and every night he said, "I really ought to have thought of something." But he never could think of anything to take away the fear of the gentle islanders.

It was on the sixth night that the storm came. The wind blew and the sea roared and the castle shook to its very foundations. And Philip, awakened by the noise and the shaking, sat up in bed and understood what the fear was that spoiled the happiness of the Dwellers by the Sea.

"Suppose the sea did sweep us all away," he said. "And they haven't even got a boat."

And then, when he was quite far from expecting it, he did think of something. And he went on thinking about it so hard that he couldn't sleep anymore.

And in the morning he said to the parrot:

"I've thought of something. And I'm not going to tell the others. But I can't do it all by myself. Do you think you could get Perrin for me?"

"I will try with pleasure," replied the obliging bird, and flew off without further speech.

That afternoon, just as a picnic tea was ending, a great shadow fell on the party, and next moment the Hippogriff alighted with Mr. Perrin and the parrot on its back.

"Oh, *thank* you," said Philip, and led Mr. Perrin away and began to talk to him in whispers.

"No, sir," Mr. Perrin answered suddenly and aloud. "I'm sorry, but I couldn't think of it."

"Don't you know *how*?" Philip asked.

"I know everything as is to be known in my trade," said Mr. Perrin, "but carpentry's one thing, and manners is another. Not but what I know manners too, which is why I won't be a party to no such a thing."

"But you don't understand," said Philip, trying to keep up with Mr. Perrin's long strides. "What I want to do is for you to build a Noah's ark on the top of the highest tower. Then when the sea's rough and the wind blows, all the Sea-Dwellers can just get into their ark and then they'll be quite safe whatever happens."

"You said all that afore," said Mr. Perrin, "and I wonder at you, so I do."

"I thought it was *such* a good idea," said poor Philip in gloom.

"Oh, the *idea's* all right," said Mr. Perrin. "There ain't nothing to complain of 'bout the *idea*."

"Then what *is* wrong?" Philip asked impatiently.

"You've come to the wrong shop," said Mr. Perrin slowly. "I ain't the man to take away another chap's job, not if he was to be in the humblest way of business; but when it comes to slapping the government in the face, well, there, Master Pip, I wouldn't have thought it of you. It's as much as my place is worth."

"Look here," said Philip, stopping short in despair, "will you tell me straight out why you won't help me?"

"I'm not a-going to go building arks, at my time of life," said Mr. Perrin. "Mr. Noah'd break his old heart, so he would, if I was to take on his job over his head."

"Oh, you mean I ought to ask him?"

"'Course you ought to ask him. I don't mind lending a hand under his directions, acting as foreman like, so as to make a good job of it. But it's him you must give your order to."

The parrot and the Hippogriff between them managed to get Mr. Noah to the castle by noon of the next day.

"Would you have minded," Philip immediately asked him, "if I'd had an ark built without asking you to do it?"

"Well," said Mr. Noah mildly, "I might have been a little hurt. I have had some experience, you know, my Lord."

"Why do you call me that?" Philip asked.

"Because you are, of course. Your deed of slaying the lions counts one to you, and by virtue of it you are now a Baron. I congratulate you, Lord Leo," said Mr. Noah.

He approved of Philip's idea, and he and Perrin were soon busy making plans, calculating strains and selecting materials.

Then Philip made a speech to the islanders and explained his idea. There was a great deal of cheering and shouting, and everyone agreed that an ark on the topmost tower would meet a longfelt want, and that when once that ark was there, fear would forever be a stranger to every gentle island heart.

And now the great work of building began. Mr. Perrin kindly consented to act as foreman and set to work a whole army of workmen—the M.A.'s of course. And soon the sound of saw and hammer mingled with the plash of waves and cries of seabirds, and gangs of stalwart M.A.'s in their seaweed tunics bent themselves to the task of shaping great timbers and hoisting them to the top of the highest tower, where other gangs, under Mr. Noah's own eye, reared a scaffolding to support the ark while the building went on.

The children were not allowed to help, but they loved looking on, and almost felt that if they looked on earnestly enough, they must, in some strange mysterious way, be actually helping. You know the feeling, I daresay.

The Hippogriff, who was stabled in the castle, flew up to wherever he was wanted, to assist in the hauling. Mr. Noah only had to whisper the magic word in his ear and up he flew. But what that magic word was the children did not know, though they asked often enough.

And now at last the ark was finished, the scaffolding was removed, and there was the great Noah's ark, firmly planted on the topmost tower. It was a perfect example of the ark builder's craft. Its boat part was painted a dull red, its sides and ends were blue with black windows, and its roof was bright scarlet, painted in lines to imitate tiles. No least detail was neglected. Even to the white bird painted on the roof, which you must have noticed in your own Noah's ark.

A great festival was held, speeches were made, and everyone who had lent a hand in the building, even the humblest M.A., was crowned with a wreath of fresh pink-and-green seaweed. Songs were sung, and the laureate of the Sea-Dwellers, a young M.A. with pale blue eyes and no chin, recited an ode beginning:

"Now that we have our Noble Ark
No more we tremble in the dark
When the great seas and the winds cry out,
For we are safe without a doubt.

At undue risings of the tide
Within our Ark we'll safely hide,

*They loved looking on.*

And bless the names of those who thus
Have built a painted Ark for us."

There were three hundred and seventeen more lines, very much like these, and everyone said it was wonderful, and the laureate was a genius, and how did he do it, and what brains, eh? and things like that.

And Philip and Lucy had crowns too. The Lord High Islander made a vote of thanks to Philip, who modestly replied that it was nothing, really, and anybody could have done it. And a spirit of gladness spread about among the company so that everyone was smiling and shaking hands with everybody else, and even the M.A.'s were making little polite old jokes, and slapping each other on the back and calling each other "old chap," which was not at all their habit in ordinary life. The whole castle was decorated with garlands of pink and green seaweed like the wreaths that people were wearing, and the whole scene was the gayest and happiest you can imagine.

And then the dreadful thing happened.

Philip and Lucy were standing in their seaweed tunics, for of course they had, since the first day, worn the costume of the country, on the platform in the courtyard. Mr. Noah had just said, "Well, then, we will enjoy this enjoyable day to the very end and return to the city tomorrow," when a shadow fell on the group. It was the Hippogriff, and on its back was—someone. Before anyone could see who that someone was, the Hippogriff had flown low enough for that someone to catch Philip by his seaweed tunic and to swing him off his feet and onto the Hippogriff's back. Lucy screamed, Mr. Perrin said, "Here, I say, none of that," and Mr. Noah said, "Dear me!" And they all reached out their hands to pull Philip back. But they were all too late.

"I won't go. Put me down," Philip shouted. They all heard that. And also they heard the answer of the person on the Hippogriff—the person who had snatched Philip onto its back.

"Oh, won't you, my lord? We'll soon see about that," the person said.

132

Three people there knew that voice, four counting Philip, six counting the dogs. The dogs barked and growled, Mr. Noah said, "Drop it," and Lucy screamed, "Oh no! Oh no! It's that Pretenderette." The parrot, with great presence of mind, flew up into the air and attacked the ear of the Pretenderette, for, as old books say, it was indeed that unprincipled character who had broken from prison and once more stolen the Hippogriff. But the Pretenderette was not to be caught twice by the same parrot. She was ready for the bird this time, and as it touched her ear she caught it in her motor veil, which she must have loosened beforehand, and thrust it into a wicker cage that hung ready from the saddle of the Hippogriff, who hovered on his wide white wings above the crowd of faces upturned.

"Now we shall see her face," Lucy thought, for she could not get rid of the feeling that if she could only see the Pretenderette's face she would recognize it. But the Pretenderette was too wily to look down unveiled. She turned her face up, and she must have whispered the magic word, for the Hippogriff rose in the air and began to fly away with incredible swiftness across the sea.

"Oh, what shall I do?" cried Lucy, wringing her hands. You have often heard of people wringing their hands. Lucy, I assure you, really did wring hers. "Oh! Mr. Noah, what will she do with him? Where will she take him? What shall I do? How can I find him again?"

"I deeply regret, my dear child," said Mr. Noah, "that I find myself quite unable to answer any single one of your questions."

"But can't I go after him?" Lucy persisted.

"I am sorry to say," said Mr. Noah, "that we have no boats, the Pretenderette has stolen our one and only Hippogriff, and none of our camels can fly."

"But what can I *do*?" Lucy stamped her foot in her agony of impatience.

"Nothing, my child," Mr. Noah aggravatingly replied, "except to go to bed and get a good night's rest. Tomorrow we will return to the city and see what can be done. We must consult the oracle."

"But can't we go *now?*" said Lucy, crying.

"No oracle is worth consulting till it's had its night's rest," said Mr. Noah. "It is a three days' journey. If we started now—see it is already dusk—we should arrive in the middle of the night. We will start early in the morning."

But early in the morning there was no starting from the castle of the Dwellers by the Sea. There was indeed no one to start, and there was no castle to start from.

A young blugraiwee, peeping out of its hole after a rather disturbed night to see whether any human beings were yet stirring or whether it might venture out in search of yellow periwinkles, which are its favorite food, started, pricked its spotted ears, looked again, and, disdaining the cover of the rocks, walked boldly out across the beach. For the beach was deserted. There was no one there. No Mr. Noah, no Lucy, no gentle islanders, no M.A.'s—and what is more there were no huts and there was no castle. All was smooth, plain, bare seacombed beach.

For the sea had at last risen. The fear of the Dwellers had been justified. Whether the sea had been curious about the ark no one knows, no one will ever know. At any rate the sea had risen up and swept away from the beach every trace of the castle, the huts and the folk who had lived there.

A bright parrot, with a streamer of motor veiling hanging to one claw, called suddenly from the clear air to the little blugraiwee.

"What's up?" the parrot asked. "Where's everything got to?"

"I don't know, I'm sure," said the little blugraiwee, "these human things are always coming and going. Have some periwinkles? They're very fine this morning after the storm," it said.

# CHAPTER EIGHT

## Ups and Downs

WE LEFT Lucy in tears and Philip in the grasp of the hateful Pretenderette, who, seated on the Hippogriff, was bearing him away across the smooth blueness of the wide sea.

"Oh, Mr. Noah," said Lucy, between sniffs and sobs, "how *can* she! You *did* say the Hippogriff could only carry one!"

"One ordinary human being," said Mr. Noah gently. "You forget that dear Philip is now an earl."

"But do you really think he's safe?" Lucy asked.

"Yes," said Mr. Noah. "And now, dear Lucy, no more questions. Since your arrival on our shores I have been gradually growing more accustomed to being questioned, but I still find it unpleasant and fatiguing. Desist, I entreat."

So Lucy desisted and everyone went to bed, and, for crying is very tiring, to sleep. But not for long.

Lucy was awakened in her bed of soft dry seaweed by the sound of the castle alarm bell, and by the blaring of trumpets and the shouting of many voices. A bright light shone in at the window of her room. She jumped up and ran to the window and leaned out. Below lay the

135

great courtyard of the castle, a moving sea of people on which hundreds of torches seemed to float, and the sound of shouting rose in the air as foam rises in the wind.

"The Fear! The Fear!" people were shouting. "To the ark! To the ark!" And the black night that pressed around the castle was loud with the wild roar of waves and the shriek of a tumultuous wind.

Lucy ran to the door of her room. But suddenly she stopped.

"My clothes," she said. And dressed herself hastily. For she perceived that her own petticoats and shoes were likely to have better wearing qualities than seaweed could possess, and if they were all going to take refuge in the ark, she felt she would rather have her own clothes on.

"Mr. Noah is sure to come for me," she most sensibly told herself. "And I'll get as many clothes on as I can." Her own dress, of course, had been left at Polistopolis, but the ballet dress would be better than the seaweed tunic. When she was dressed she ran into Philip's room and rolled his clothes into a little bundle and carried it under her arm as she ran down the stairs. Halfway down she met Mr. Noah coming up.

"Ah! You're ready," he said. "It is well. Do not be alarmed, my Lucy. The tide is rising but slowly. There will be time for everyone to escape. All is in train, and the embarkation of the animals is even now in progress. There has been a little delay in sorting the beasts into pairs. But we are getting on. The Lord High Islander is showing remarkable qualities. All the big animals are on board; the pigs were being coaxed on as I came up. And the anteaters are having a late supper. Do not be alarmed."

"I can't help being alarmed," said Lucy, slipping her free hand into Mr. Noah's, "but I won't cry or be silly. Oh, I do wish Philip was here."

"Most unreasonable of girl children," said Mr. Noah. "We are in danger and you wish him to be here to share it?"

"Oh, we *are* in danger, are we?" said Lucy quickly. "I thought you said I wasn't to be alarmed."

"No more you are," said Mr. Noah shortly. "Of course you're in danger. But there's me. And there's the ark. What more do you want?"

"Nothing," Lucy answered in a very small voice, and the two made their way to a raised platform overlooking the long inclined road that led up to the tower on which the ark had been built. A long procession toiled slowly up it of animals in pairs, urged and goaded by the M.A.'s under the orders of the Lord High Islander.

The wild wind blew the flames of the torches out like golden streamers, and the sound of the waves was like thunder on the shore.

Down below other M.A.'s were busy carrying bales tied up in seaweed. Seen from above the busy figures looked like ants when you kick into an anthill and the little ant people run this way and that way and every way about their little ant businesses.

The Lord High Islander came in pale and serious, with all the calm competence of Napoleon at a crisis.

"Sorry to have to worry you, sir," he said to Mr. Noah, "but of course your experience is invaluable just now. I can't remember what bears eat. Is it hay or meat?"

"It's buns," said Lucy. "I beg your pardon, Mr. Noah. Of course, I ought to have waited for you to say."

"In my ark," said Mr. Noah, "buns were unknown and bears were fed entirely on honey, the providing of which kept our pair of bees fully employed. But if you are sure bears *like* buns we must always be humane, dear Lucy, and study the natural taste of the animals in our charge."

"They love them," said Lucy.

"Buns and honey," said the Lord Islander. "And what about bats?"

"I don't know what bats eat," said Mr. Noah. "I believe it was settled after some discussion that they don't eat cats. But what they *do* eat is one of the eleven mysteries. You had better let the bats fast."

"They *are*, sir," said the Lord High Islander.

"And is all going well? Shall I come down and lend a personal eye?"

"I think I'm managing all right, sir," said the Lord High Islander

*A long procession toiled slowly up it of animals in pairs.*

modestly. "You see, it's a great honor for me. The M.A.'s are carrying in the provisions, the boys are stowing them and also herding the beasts. They are very good workers, sir."

"Are you frightened?" Lucy whispered, as he turned to go back to his overseeing.

"Not I," said the Lord High Islander. "Don't you understand that I've been promoted to be Lord Vice-Noah of Polistarchia? And of course the hearts of all Vice-Noahs are strangers to fear. But just think what a difficult thing fear would have been to be a stranger to if you and Philip hadn't got us the ark!"

"It was Philip's doing," said Lucy. "Oh, *do* you think he's all right?"

"I think his heart is a stranger to fear, naturally," said the Lord High Islander, "so he's certain to be all right."

When the last of the animals had sniffed and sniveled its way into the ark—it was a porcupine with a cold in its head—the islanders, the M.A.'s, Lucy, and Mr. Noah followed. And when everyone was in, the door of the ark was shut from inside by an ingenious mechanical contrivance worked by a more than usually intelligent M.A.

You must not suppose that the inside of the ark was anything like the inside of your own Noah's ark, where all the animals are put in anyhow, all mixed together and wrong way up as likely as not. That, with live animals and live people, would, as you will readily imagine, be quite uncomfortable. The inside of the ark which had been built under the direction of Mr. Noah and Mr. Perrin was not at all like that. It was more like the inside of a big Atlantic liner than anything else I can think of. All the animals were stowed away in suitable stalls, and there were delightful cabins for all those for whom cabins were suitable. The islanders and the M.A.'s retired to their cabins in perfect order, and Lucy and Mr. Noah, Mr. Perrin and the Lord High Islander gathered in the saloon, which was large and had walls and doors of inlaid mother-of-pearl and pink coral. It was lighted by glass globes filled with phosphorus collected by an ingenious process invented by another of the M.A.'s.

"And now," said Mr. Noah, "I beg that anxiety may be dismissed from every mind. If the waters subside, they leave us safe. If they rise, as I confidently expect them to do, our ark will float, and we still are safe. In the morning I will take soundings and begin to steer a course. We will select a suitable spot on the shore, land, and proceed to the Hidden Places, where we will consult the oracle. A little refreshment before we retire for what is left of the night? A captain's biscuit would perhaps not be inappropriate?" He took a tin from a locker and handed it round.

"That's A1, sir," said the Lord High Islander, munching. "What a head you have for the right thing."

"All practice," said Mr. Noah modestly.

"Thank you," said Lucy, taking a biscuit. "I wish—"

The sentence was never finished. With a sickening suddenness the floor of the saloon heaved up under their feet, a roaring, surging, battering sound broke round them, the saloon tipped over on one side, and the whole party was thrown on the pink silk cushions of the long settee. A shudder seemed to run through the ark from end to end, and "What is it? Oh! What is it?" cried Lucy as the ark heeled over the other way and the unfortunate occupants were thrown onto the opposite set of cushions. (It really *was*, now, rather like what you imagine the inside of your Noah's ark must be when you put in Mr. Noah and his family and a few hastily chosen animals and shake them all up together.)

"It's the sea," cried the Lord High Islander, "it's the great Fear come upon us! And I'm not afraid!" He drew himself up as well as he could in his cramped position, with Mr. Noah's elbow pinning his shoulder down and Mr. Perrin's boot on his ear.

With a shake and a shiver the ark righted itself, and the floor of the saloon got flat again.

"It's all right," said Mr. Perrin, resuming control of his boot. "Good workmanship, it do tell. She ain't shipped a drop, Mr. Noah, sir."

"It's all right," said Mr. Noah, taking his elbow to himself and standing up rather shakily on his yellow mat.

> "We're afloat, we're afloat
> > On the dark rolling tide;
> The ark's watertight
> > And the crew are inside.

> "Up, up with the flag
> > Let it wave o'er the sea;
> We're afloat, we're afloat—
> > And what else should we be?"

"*I* don't know," said Lucy, "but there isn't any flag, is there?"

"The principle's the same," said Mr. Noah, "but I'm afraid we didn't think of a flag."

"*I* did," said Mr. Perrin. "It's only a Jubilee hankey"—he drew it slowly from his breast pocket, a cotton Union Jack it was—"but it shall wave all right. But not till daylight, I think, sir. Discretion's the better part of—don't you think, Mr. Noah, sir? Wouldn't do to open the ark out of hours, so to speak!"

"Just so," said Mr. Noah. "One, two, three! Bed!"

The ark swayed easily on a sea not too rough. The saloon passengers staggered to their cabins. And silence reigned in the ark.

\* \* \* \* \* \*

I am sorry to say that the Pretenderette dropped the wicker cage containing the parrot into the sea—an unpardonable piece of cruelty and revenge; unpardonable, that is, unless you consider that she did not really know any better. The Hippogriff's white wings swept on; Philip, now laid across the knees of the Pretenderette (a most undignified attitude for any boy, and I hope none of you may be placed in such a position), screamed as the cage struck the water, and, "Oh, Polly!" he cried.

"All right," the parrot answered. "Keep your pecker up!"

"What did it say?" the Pretenderette asked.

"Something about peck," said Philip upside down.

"Ah!" said the Pretenderette with satisfaction, "he won't do anymore pecking for some time to come." And the wide Hippogriff wings swept on over the wide sea.

Polly's cage fell and floated. And it floated alone till the dawn, when, with wheelings and waftings and cries, the gulls came from far and near to see what this new strange thing might be that bobbed up and down in their waters in the light of the newborn day.

"Hullo!" said Polly in bird-talk, clinging upside down to the top bars of the cage.

"Hullo, yourself," replied the eldest gull, "what's up? And who are you? And what are you doing in that unnatural lobster pot?"

"I conjure you," said the parrot earnestly, "I conjure you by our common birdhood to help me in my misfortune."

"No gull who *is* a gull can resist that appeal," said the master of the seabirds. "What can we do, brother-bird?"

"The matter is urgent," said Polly, but quite calmly. "I am getting very wet and I dislike saltwater. It is bad for my plumage. May I give an order to your followers, bird-brother?"

"Give," said the master gull, with a graceful wheel and whirl of his splendid wings.

"Let four of my brothers raise this detested trap high above the waves," said the parrot, "and let others of you, with your brave strong beaks, break through the bars and set me free."

"Delighted," said the master gull, "any little thing, you know," and his own high-bred beak was the first to take hold of the cage, which presently the gulls lifted in the air and broke through, setting the parrot free.

"Thank you, brother-birds," the parrot said, shaking wet wings and spreading them. "One good turn deserves another. The beach yonder was white with cockles but yesterday."

"Thank you, brother-bird," they all said, and flew fleetly cockleward.

And that was how the parrot got free from the cage and went back to the shore to have that little talk with the blugraiwee which I told you about in the last chapter.

*   *   *   *   *   *

The ark was really very pleasant by daylight with the sun shining in at its windows. The sun shone outside as well, of course, and the Union Jack waved cheerfully in the wind. Breakfast was served on the terrace at the end of the ark—you know—that terrace where the boat part turns up. It was a very nice breakfast, and the sea was quite smooth—a quite perfect sea. This was rather fortunate, for there was nothing else. Sea on every side of the ark. No land at all.

"However shall we find the way," Lucy asked the Lord High Islander, "with nothing but sea?"

"Oh," he answered, "that's all the better, really. Mr. Noah steers much better when there's no land in sight. It's all practice, you know."

"And when we come in sight of land, will he steer badly then?"

"Oh, anybody can steer then," said Billy, "you if you like." So it was Lucy who steered the ark into harbor, under Mr. Noah's directions. Arks are very easy to steer if you only know the way. Of course arks are not like other vessels; they require neither sails nor steam engines, nor oars to make them move. The very arkishness of the ark makes it move just as the steersman wishes. He only has to say "Port," "Starboard," "Right ahead," "Slow," and so on, and the ark (unlike many people I know) immediately does as it is told. So steering was easy and pleasant; one just had to keep the ark's nose toward the distant domes and pinnacles of a town that shone and glittered on the shore a few miles away. And the town grew nearer and nearer, and the black streak that was the people of the town began to show white dots that were the people's faces. And then the ark was moored against a quay side, and a friendly populace cheered as Mr. Noah stepped onto firm land, to be welcomed by the governor of the town and a choice selection of eminent citizens.

"It's quite an event for them," said Mr. Perrin. "They don't have much happening here. A very lazy lot they be, almost as bad as Somnolentia."

"What makes them lazy?" Lucy asked.

"It's owing to the onions and potatoes growing wild in these parts, I believe," said the Lord High Islander. "They get enough to eat without working. And the onions make them sleepy."

They talked apart while Mr. Noah was arranging things with the Governor of the town, who had come down to the harbor in a hurry and a flurry and a furry gown.

"I've arranged everything," said Mr. Noah at last. "The islanders and the M.A.'s and the animals are to be allowed to camp in the public park till we've consulted the oracle and decided what's to be done with them. They must live somewhere, I suppose. Life has become much too eventful for me lately. However, there are only three more deeds for the Earl of Ark to do, and then perhaps we shall have a little peace and quietness."

"The Earl of Ark?" Lucy repeated.

"Philip, you know. I do wish you'd try to remember that he's an earl now. Now you and I must take camel and be off."

And now came seven long days of camel traveling, through desert and forest and over hill and through valley, till at last Lucy and Mr. Noah came to the Hidden Place where the oracle is, and where that is I may not tell you—because it's one of the eleven mysteries. And I must not tell you what the oracle is because that is another of the mysteries. But I may tell you that if you want to consult the oracle you have to go a long way between rows of round pillars, rather like those in Egyptian tombs. And as you go it gets darker and darker, and when it is quite dark you see a little, little light a very long way off, and you hear very far away a beautiful music, and you smell the scent of flowers that do not grow in any wood or field or garden of this earth. Mixed with this scent is the scent of incense and of old tapestried rooms, where no one has lived for a very long time. And you remember all the sad and beautiful things you have ever seen or heard, and you fall down on the ground and hide your face in your hands and call on the oracle, and if you are the right sort of person the oracle answers you.

Lucy and Mr. Noah waited in the dark for the voice of the oracle, and at last it spoke. Lucy heard no words, only the most beautiful voice in the world speaking softly, and so sweetly and finely and bravely that at once she felt herself brave enough to dare any danger, and strong enough to do any deed that might be needed to get Philip out of the clutches of the base Pretenderette. All the tiredness of her long journey faded away, and but for the thought that Philip needed her, she would have been content to listen forever to that golden voice. Everything else in the world faded away and grew to seem worthless and unmeaning. Only the soft golden voice remained and the gray hard voice that said, "You've got to look after Philip, you know!" And the two voices together made a harmony more beautiful than you will find in any of Beethoven's sonatas. Because Lucy knew that she should follow the gray voice, and remember the golden voice as long as she lived.

But something was tiresomely pulling at her sleeve, dragging her away from the wonderful golden voice. Mr. Noah was pulling her sleeve and saying, "Come away," and they turned their backs on the little light and the music and the enchanting perfumes, and instantly the voice stopped and they were walking between dusky pillars toward a far gray speck of sunlight.

It was not till they were once more under the bare sky that Lucy said, "What did it say?"

"You must have heard," said Mr. Noah.

"I only heard the voice and what it meant. I didn't understand the words. But the voice was like dreams and everything beautiful I've ever thought of."

"I thought it a wonderfully straightforward businesslike oracle," said Mr. Noah briskly, "and the voice was quite distinct and I remember every word it said."

(Which just shows how differently the same thing may strike two people.)

"What did it say?" Lucy asked, trotting along beside him, still clutching Philip's bundle, which through all these days she had never let go.

And Mr. Noah gravely recited the following lines. I agree with him that, for an oracle, they were extremely straightforward.

> "You had better embark
> Once again in the Ark,
> And sailing from dry land
> Make straight for the Island."

"Did it *really* say that?" Lucy asked.

"Of course it did," said Mr. Noah. "That's a special instruction to me, but I daresay you heard something quite different. The oracle doesn't say the same thing to everyone, of course. Didn't you get any special instruction?

"Only to try to be brave and good," said Lucy shyly.

"Well, then," said Mr. Noah, "you carry out your instructions and I'll carry out mine."

"But what's the use of going to the island if you can't land when you get there?" Lucy insisted. "You know only two people can land there, and we're not them, are we?"

"Oh, if you begin asking what's the use, we shan't get anywhere," said Mr. Noah. "And more than half the things you say are questions."

\*　　\*　　\*　　\*　　\*　　\*

I'm sorry this chapter is cut up into bits with lines of stars, but stars are difficult to avoid when you have to tell about a lot of different things happening all at once. That is why it is much better always to keep your party together if you can. And I have allowed mine to get separated so that Philip, the parrot, and the rest of the company are going through three sets of adventures all at the same time. This is most trying for me, and fully accounts for the stars. Which I hope you'll excuse. However.

We now come back by way of the stars to Philip wrong way up in the clutches of the Pretenderette. She had breathed the magic word in the Hippogriff's ear, but she had not added any special order. So the Hippogriff was entirely its own master as far as the choice of where it was to go was concerned. It tossed its white mane after circling three times between air and sky, made straight for the Island-where-you-mayn't-go. The Pretenderette didn't know that it was the Island-where-you-mayn't-go, and as they got nearer and she could see plainly its rainbow-colored sands, its palms, and its waterfalls, its cool green thickets and many tinted flowers and glowing fruits, it seemed to her that she might do worse than land there and rest for a little while. For even the most disagreeable people get tired sometimes, and the Pretenderette had had a hard day of it. So she made no attempt to check the Hippogriff or alter its course. And when the Hippogriff was hovering but a few inches from the grass of the most beautiful of the island glades, she jerked Philip roughly off her knee and he fell all in a heap on the ground. With great presence of mind our hero—if he isn't a hero by now he never will be—picked himself up and bolted into the bushes. No rabbit could have bolted more instantly and fleetly.

"I'll teach you," said the furious Pretenderette, preparing to alight. She looked down to find a soft place to jump on. And then she saw that every blade of grass was a tiny spear of steel, and every spear was pointed at her. She made the Hippogriff take her to another glade—more little steel spears. To the rainbow sands—but on looking at them she saw that they were quivering quicksands. Wherever green grass had grown the spears now grew and wherever the sand was it was a terrible trap of quicksand. She tried to dismount in a little pool, but fortunately for her she noticed in time that what shone in it so silvery was not water but white-hot molten metal.

"What a nasty place," said the Pretenderette. "I don't know that I could have chosen a nastier place to leave that naughty child in. He'll know who's master by the time I send to fetch him back to prison. Here, you, get back to Polistopolis as fast as you can. See? Please, I mean," she added, and then she spoke the magic word.

Philip was peeping through the bushes close by, and he heard that magic word (I dare not tell you what it is) and he saw for the first time the face of the Pretenderette. And he trembled and shivered in his bushy lurking place. For the Pretenderette was the only really unpleasant person Philip had ever met in the world. It was Lucy's nurse, the nurse with the gray dress and the big fat feet, who had been so cross to him and had pulled down his city.

"How on earth," Philip wondered to himself, "did she get *here*? And how on earth shall I get away from her?" He had not seen the spears and the quicksands and the molten metal, and he was waiting unhappily for her to alight, and for a game of hide-and-seek to begin, which he was not at all anxious to play.

Even as he wondered, the Hippogriff spread wings and flew away. And Philip was left alone on the island. But what did that matter? It was much better to be alone than with that Pretenderette. And for Philip there were no white-hot metal and spears and snares of quicksand, only dewy grass and sweet flowers and trees and safety and delight.

"If only Lucy were here," he said.

When he was quite sure that the Pretenderette was really gone, he came out and explored the island. It had on it every kind of flower and fruit that you can think of, all growing together. There were gold oranges and white orange flowers, pink apple blossom and red apples, cherries and cherry blossom, strawberry flowers and strawberries, all growing together, wild and sweet.

At the back of his mind Philip remembered that he had, at some time or other, heard of an island where fruit and blossoms grew together at the same time, but that was all he could remember. He passed through the lovely orchards and came to a lake. It was frozen. And he remembered that, in the island he had heard of, there was a lake ready for skating even when the flowers and fruit were on the trees. Then he came to a little summer house built all of porcupine quills like Helen's pen box.

And then he knew. All these wonders were on the island that he and Helen had invented long ago—the island that she used to draw maps of.

"It's our very own island," he said, and a glorious feeling of being at home glowed through him, warm and delightful. "We said no one else might come here! That's why the Pretenderette couldn't land. And why they call it the Island-where-you-mayn't-go. I'll find the bun tree and have something to eat, and then I'll go to the boathouse and get out the *Lightning Loose* and go back for Lucy. I do wish I could bring her here. But of course I can't without asking Helen."

The *Lightning Loose* was the magic yacht Helen had invented for the island.

He soon found a bush whose fruit was buns, and a jam-tart tree grew near it. You have no idea how nice jam tarts can taste till you have gathered them yourself, fresh and sticky, from the tree. They are as sticky as horse chestnut buds, and much nicer to eat.

As he went toward the boathouse he grew happier and happier, recognizing, one after the other, all the places he and Helen had planned and marked on the map. He passed by the marble and gold house with "King's Palace" painted on the door. He longed to explore it but the thought of Lucy drove him on. As he went down a narrow leafy woodland path toward the boathouse, he passed the door of the dear little thatched cottage (labeled "Queen's Palace") which was the house Helen had insisted that she liked best for her very own.

"How pretty it is; I wish Helen were here," he said. "She helped to make it. I should never have thought of it without her. She ought to be here," he said. With that he felt very lonely, all of a sudden, and

*Walked straight into the arms of—Helen*

very sad. And as he went on, wondering whether in all this magic world there might not somehow be some magic strong enough to bring Helen there to see the island that was their very own, and to give her consent to his bringing Lucy to it, he turned a corner in the woodland path, and walked straight into the arms of—Helen.

CHAPTER NINE

# On the "Lightning Loose"

"BUT HOW did you get here?" said Philip in Helen's arms on the island.

"I just walked out at the other side of a dream," she said. "How could I not come, when the door was open and you wanted me so?"

And Philip just said, "Oh, Helen!" He could not find any other words, but Helen understood. She always did.

"Come," she said, "shall we go to your palace or mine? I want my supper, and we'll have our own little blue-and-white tea set. Yes, I know you've had your supper, but it'll be fun getting mine, and perhaps you'll be hungry again before we've got it."

They went to the thatched cottage that was Helen's palace, because Philip had had almost as much of large buildings as he wanted for a little while. The cottage had a wide chimney and an open hearth; and they sat on the hearth and made toast, and Philip almost forgot that he had ever had any adventures and that the toast was being made on a hearth whose blue wood smoke curled up among the enchanting treetops of a magic island.

And before they went to bed he had told her all about everything.

"Oh, I am so glad you came!" he said over and over again. "It is so easy to tell you *here*, with all the magic going on. I don't think I ever *could* have told you at the Grange with the servants all about, and the—I mean Mr. Graham, and all the things as not magic as they could possibly be. Oh, Helen! Where is Mr. Graham; won't he hate your coming away from him?"

"He's gone through a dream door too," she said, "to see Lucy. Only he doesn't know he's really gone. He'll think it's a dream, and he'll tell me about it when we both wake up."

"When did you go to sleep?" said Philip.

"At Brussels. That telegram hasn't come yet."

"I don't understand about time," said Philip firmly, "and I never shall. I say, Helen, I was just looking for the *Lightning Loose*, to go off in her on a voyage of discovery and find Lucy."

"I don't think you need," she said. "I met a parrot on the island just before I met you and it was saying poetry to itself."

"It would be," said Philip, "if it was alive. I'm glad it is alive, though. What was it saying?"

"It was something like this," she said, putting a log of wood on the fire:

> "Philip and Helen
> Have the island to dwell in,
>> Hooray.
> They said of the island,
> "It's your land and my land"
>> Hooray.  Hooray.  Hooray.
>
> "And till the ark
> Comes out of the dark
> There those two may stay
> For a happy while, and
> Enjoy their island

Until the Giving Day.
>Hooray.

"And then they will hear the giving voice,
They will hear and obey,
And when people come
Who need a home,
They'll give the island away.
>Hooray.

"The island with flower
And fruit and bower,
Forest and river and bay,
Their very own island
They'll sigh and smile and
They'll give their island away."

"What nonsense!" said Philip. "I never will."

"All right, my Pipkin," said Helen cheerfully. "I only told you just to show that you're expected to stay here. Philip and Helen have the island to dwell in. And now, what about bed?"

They spent a whole week on the island. It was exactly all that they could wish an island to be; because, of course, they had made it themselves, and, of course, they knew exactly what they wanted. I can't describe that week. I only know that Philip will never forget it. Just think of all the things you could do on a magic island if you were there with your dearest dear, and you'll know how Philip spent his time.

He enjoyed every minute of every hour of every day, and, best thing of all, that week made him understand, as nothing else could have done, that Helen still belonged to him, and that her marriage to Mr. Graham had not made her any the less Philip's very own Helen.

And then came a day when Philip, swinging in a magnolia tree, looked out to sea and cried out, "A sail! A sail! Oh, Helen, here's the ark! Now it's all over. Let's have Lucy to stay with us, and send the other people away," he added, sliding down the tree trunk with his face very serious.

"But we can't, dear," Helen reminded him. "The island's ours, you know; and as long as it's ours no one else can land on it. We made it like that, you know."

"Then they can't land?"

"No," said Helen.

"Can't we change the rule and let them land?"

"No," said Helen.

"Oh, it is a pity," Philip said, "because the island is the place for islanders, isn't it?"

"Yes," said Helen, "and there's no fear of the sea here; you remember we made it like that when we made the island?"

"Yes," said Philip. "Oh, Helen, I *don't* want to."

"Then don't," said Helen.

"Ah, but I *do* want to, too."

"Then do," said she.

"But don't you see, when you want to and don't want to at the same time, what *are* you to do? There are so many things to think of."

"When it's like that, there's one thing you mustn't think of," she said.

"What?" Philip asked.

"Yourself," she said softly.

There was a silence, and then Philip suddenly hugged his sister and she hugged him.

"I'll give it to them," he said, "it's no use. I know I ought to. I shall only be uncomfortable if I don't."

Helen laughed. "My boy of boys!" she said. And then she looked sad. "Boy of my heart," she said, "you know it's not only giving up our island. If we give it away I must go. It's the only place that there's a door into out of my dreams."

"I can't let you go," he said.

155

"But you've got your deeds to do," she said, "and I can't help you in those. Lucy can help you, but I can't. You like Lucy now, don't you?"

"Oh, I don't mind her," said Philip, "but it's *you* I want, Helen."

"Don't think about that," she urged. "Think what the islanders want. Think what it'll be to them to have the island, to live here always, safe from the fear!"

"There are three more deeds," said Philip dismally. "I don't think I shall ever want any more adventures as long as I live."

"You'll always want them," she said, laughing at him gently, "always. And now let's do the thing handsomely and give them a splendid welcome. Give me a kiss and then we'll gather heaps of roses."

So they kissed each other. But Philip was very unhappy indeed, though he felt that he was being rather noble and that Helen thought so too, which was naturally a great comfort.

There had been a good deal more of this talk than I have set down. Philip and Helen had hardly had time to hang garlands of pink roses along the quayside where the *Lightning Loose*, that perfect yacht, lay at anchor, before the blunt prow of the ark bumped heavily against the quayside—and the two, dropping the rest of the roses, waved and smiled to the group on the ark's terrace.

The first person to speak was Mr. Perrin, who shouted, "Here we are again!" like a clown.

Then Lucy said, "We know we can't land, but the oracle said come and we came." She leaned over the bulwark to whisper, "Who's that perfect duck you've got with you?"

Philip answered aloud:

"This is my sister, Helen—Helen, this is Lucy."

The two looked at each other, and then Helen held out her hands and she and Lucy kissed each other.

"I knew I should like you," Lucy whispered, "but I didn't know I should like you quite so much."

Mr. Noah and Mr. Perrin were both bowing to Helen, a little

stiffly but very cordially all the same, and quite surprisingly without surprise. And the Lord High Islander was looking at her with his own friendly jolly schoolboy grin.

"If you will embark," said Mr. Noah politely, "we can return to the mainland, and I will explain to you your remaining deeds."

"Tell them, Pip," said Helen.

"We don't want to embark—at present," said Philip shyly. "We want you to land."

"No one may land on the island save two," said Mr. Noah. "I am glad you are the two. I feared one of the two might be the Pretenderette."

"Not much," said Philip. "It's Helen's and mine. We made it. And we want to give it to the islanders to keep. For their very own," he added, feeling that it would be difficult for anyone to believe that such a glorious present was really being made just like that, without speeches, as if it had been a little present of a pencil sharpener or a peg top.

He was right.

"To keep?" said the Lord High Islander. "For our very own? Always?"

"Yes," said Philip. "And there's no fear here. You'll *really* be 'happy troops' now."

For a moment nobody said anything, though all the faces were expressive. Then the Lord High Islander spoke.

"Well," he said, "of all the brickish bricks—" and could say no more.

"There are lots of houses," said Philip, "and room for all the animals, and the island is thirty miles round, so there's lots of room for the animals and everything." He felt happier than he had ever done in his life. Giving presents is always enjoyable, and this was such a big and beautiful present, and he loved it so.

"I always did say Master Pip was a gentleman, and I always shall," Mr. Perrin remarked.

"I congratulate you," said Mr. Noah, "and I am happy to announce that your fifth deed is now accomplished. You remember our empty silver fruit dishes? Your fifth deed was to be the supplying of Polistarchia with fruit. This island is the only place in the kingdom where fruit grows. The ark will serve to convey the fruit to the mainland, and the performance of this deed raises you to the rank of Duke."

"Philip, you're a dear," said Lucy in a whisper.

"Shut up," said Philip fiercely.

"Three cheers," said a familiar voice, "for the Duke of Donors."

"Three cheers," repeated the Lord High Islander, "for the Duke of Donors."

What a cheer! All the islanders cheered and the M.A.'s and Lucy and Mr. Perrin and Mr. Noah, and from the inside of the ark came enthusiastic barkings and gruntings and roarings and squeakings—as the animals of course joined in as well as they could. Thousands of gulls, circling on white wings in the sun above, added their screams to the general chorus. And when the sound of the last cheer died away, a little near familiar voice said:

"Well done, Philip! I'm proud of you."

It was the parrot who, perched on the rigging of the *Lightning Loose*, had started the cheering.

"So that's all right," it said, fluttered onto Philip's shoulder, and added, "I've heard you calling for me on the island all the week. But I felt I needed a rest. I've been talking too much. And that Pretenderette. And that cage. I assure you I needed a little time to get over my adventures."

"We have all had our adventures," said Mr. Noah gently. And Helen said:

"Won't you land and take possession of the island? I'm sure we are longing to hear each other's adventures."

"You first," said Mr. Noah to the Lord High Islander, who stepped ashore very gravely.

When Helen saw him come forward, she suddenly kissed Philip, and as the Lord High Islander's foot touched the shore of that enchanted island, she simply and suddenly vanished.

"Oh!" cried Philip. "I wish I hadn't." And his mouth trembled as girls' mouths do if they are going to cry.

"The more a present costs you, the more it's worth," said Mr. Noah. "This has cost you so much, it's the most splendid present in the world."

"I know," said Philip. "Make yourselves at home, won't you?" he just managed to say. And then he found he could not say any more. He just turned and went into the forest. And when he was alone in a green glade, he flung himself down on his face and lay a long time without moving. It had been such a happy week. And he was so tired of adventures.

When at last he sniffed with an air of finality and raised his head, the first thing he saw was Lucy, sitting quite still with her back to him.

"Hullo!" he said rather crossly. "What are you doing here?"

"Saying the multiplication table," said Lucy promptly and turned her head, "so as not even to think about you. And I haven't even once turned around. I knew you wanted to be alone. But I wanted to be here when you'd done being alone. See? I've got something to say to you."

"Fire ahead," said Philip, still grumpy.

"I think you're perfectly splendid," said Lucy very seriously, "and I want it to be real pax forever. And I'll help you in the rest of the adventures. And if you're cross, I'll try not to mind. Napoleon was cross sometimes, I believe," she added pensively, "and Julius Caesar."

"Oh, that's all right," said Philip very awkwardly.

"Then we're going to be real chums?"

"Oh yes, if you like. Only—I don't mind just this once, and it was decent of you to come and sit there with your back to me—only I hate gas."

"Yes," said Lucy obediently, "I know. Only sometimes you feel you must gas a little or burst of admiration. And I've got your proper clothes in a bundle. I've been carrying them about ever since the islanders' castle was washed away. Here they are."

She produced the bundle. And this time Philip was really touched.

"Now I *do* call that something like," he said. "The seaweed dress is all right here, but you never know what you may have to go through when you're doing adventures. There might be thorns or snakes or anything. I'm jolly glad to get my boots back too. I say, come on. Let's go to Helen's palace and get a banquet ready. I know there'll have to be a banquet. There always is, here. I know a first-rate bun tree quite near here."

"The coconut-ice plants looked beautiful as I came along," said Lucy. "What a lovely island it is. And you made it!"

"No gas," said Philip warningly. "Helen and I made it."

"She's the dearest darling," said Lucy.

"Oh, well," said Philip with resignation, "if you must gas, gas about her."

The banquet was all that you can imagine of interesting and magnificent. And Philip was, of course, the hero of the hour. And when the banquet was finished and the last guest had departed to its own house—for the houses on the island were, of course, all ready to be occupied, furnished to the last point of comfort, with pincushions full of pins in every room—Mr. Noah and Lucy and Philip sat down on the terrace steps among the pink roses for a last little talk.

"Because," said Philip, "we shall start the first thing in the morning. So please will you tell me now what the next deed is that I have to do?"

"Will you go by ark?" Mr. Noah asked, rolling up his yellow mat to make an elbow rest and leaning on it. "I shall be delighted."

"I thought," said Philip, "we might go in the *Lightning Loose*. I've never sailed her yet, you know. Do you think I *could*?"

"Of course you can," said Mr. Noah, "and if not, Lucy can show you. Your charming yacht is steered on precisely the same principle as the ark. And in this land all the winds are favorable. You will find the yacht suitably provisioned. And I may add that you can go most of the way to your next deed by water—first the sea and then the river."

"And what," asked Philip, "is the next deed?"

160

"In the extreme north of Polistarchia," said Mr. Noah instructively, "lies a town called Somnolentia. It used to be called Briskford in happier days. A river then ran through the town, a rapid river that brought much gold from the mountains. The people used to work very hard to keep the channel clear of the lumps of gold which continually threatened to choke it. Their fields were then well watered and fruitful, and the inhabitants were cheerful and happy. But when the Hippogriff was let out of the book, a Great Sloth got out too. Evading all efforts to secure him, the Great Sloth journeyed northward. He is a very large and striking animal, and by some means, either fear or admiration, he obtained a complete ascendancy over the inhabitants of Briskford. He induced them to build him a temple of solid gold, and while they were doing this the riverbed became choked up and the stream was diverted into another channel far from the town. Since then the place is fallen into decay. The fields are parched and untilled. Such water as the people need for drinking is drawn by great labor from a well. Washing has become shockingly infrequent."

"Are we to teach the dirty chaps to wash?" asked Philip in disgust.

"Do not interrupt," said Mr. Noah. "You destroy the thread of my narrative. Where was I?"

"Washing infrequent," said Lucy, "but if the fields are dried up, what do they live on?"

"Pineapples," replied Mr. Noah, "which grow freely and do not need much water. Gathering these is the sole industry of this degraded people. Pineapples are not considered a fruit but a vegetable," he added hastily, seeing another question trembling on Philip's lips. "Whatever of their waking time can be spared from the gathering and eating of the pineapples is spent in singing choric songs in honor of the Great Sloth. And even this time is short, for such is his influence on the Somnolentians that when he sleeps they sleep too, and," added Mr. Noah impressively, "he sleeps almost all the time. Your deed is to devise some means of keeping the Great Sloth awake and busy. And I

*He induced them to build him a temple of solid gold.*

think you've got your work cut out. When you've disposed of the Great Sloth you can report yourself to me here. I shall remain here for some little time. I need a holiday. The parrot will accompany you. It knows its way about as well as any bird in the land. Good night. And good luck! You will excuse my not being down to breakfast."

And the next morning, dewy-early, Philip and Lucy and the parrot went aboard the yacht and loosed her from her moorings, and Lucy showed Philip how to steer, and the parrot sat on the mast and called out instructions.

They made for the mouth of a river. ("I never built a river," said Philip. "No," said the parrot, "it came out of the poetry book.") And when they were hungry they let down the anchor and went into the cabin for breakfast. And two people sprang to meet them, almost knocking Lucy down with the violence of their welcome. The two people were Max and Brenda.

"Oh, you dear dogs," Lucy cried, and Philip patted them, one with each hand, "how did you get here?"

"It was a little surprise of Mr. Noah's," said the parrot.

Max and Brenda whined and barked and gushed.

"I wish we could understand what they're saying," said Lucy.

"If you only knew the magic word that the Hippogriff obeys," said the parrot, "you could say it, and then you'd understand all animal talk. Only, of course, I mustn't tell it you. It's one of the eleven mysteries."

"But I know it," said Philip, and at once breathed the word in the tiny silky ear of Brenda and then in the longer silkier ear of Max, and instantly—

"Oh, my dears!" they heard Brenda say in a softly shrill excited voice. "Oh, my dearie dears! We *are* so pleased to see you. I'm only a poor little faithful doggy; I'm not clever, you know, but my affectionate nature makes me almost mad with joy to see my dear master and mistress again."

"Very glad to see you, sir," said Max with heavy politeness. "I hope you'll be comfortable here. There's no comfort for a dog like being with his master."

And with that he sat down and went to sleep, and the others had breakfast. It is rather fun cooking in yachts. And there was something new and charming in Brenda's delicate way of sitting up and begging and saying at the same time, "I do *hate* to bother my darling master and mistress, but if you *could* spare another *tiny* bit of bacon—oh, *thank you*, how good and generous you are!"

They sailed the yacht successfully into the river, which presently ran into the shadow of a tropical forest. Also out of a book.

"You might go on during the night," said the parrot, "if the dogs would steer under my directions. You could tie one end of a rope to their collars and another to the helm. It's easier than turning spits."

"Delighted!" said Max. "Only, of course, it's understood that we sleep through the day?"

"Of course," said everybody. So that was settled. And the children went to bed.

It was in the middle of the night that the parrot roused Philip with his usual gentle beak-touch. Then—

"Wake up," it said, "this is not the right river. It's not the right direction. Nothing's right. The ship's all wrong. I'm very much afraid someone has been opening a book and this river has got out."

Philip hurried out on deck, and by the light of the lamps from the cabin, gazed out at the banks of the river. At least he looked for them. But there weren't any banks. Instead, steep and rugged cliffs rose on each side, and overhead, instead of a starry sky, was a great arched roof of a cavern glistening with moisture and dark as a raven's feathers.

"We must turn back," said Philip. "I don't like this at all."

"Unfortunately," said the parrot, "there is no room to turn back, and the *Lightning Loose* is not constructed for going backward."

"Oh, dear," whispered Brenda, "I wish we hadn't come. Dear little dogs ought to be taken comfortable care of and not be sent out on nasty ships that can't turn back when it's dangerous."

"My dear," said Max with slow firmness, "dear little dogs can't help themselves now. So they had better look out for chances of helping their masters."

"But what can we *do*, then?" said Philip impatiently.

"I fear," said the parrot, "that we can do nothing but go straight on. If this river is in a book it will come out somewhere. No river in a book ever runs underground and stays there."

"I shan't wake Lucy," said Philip. "She might be frightened."

"You needn't," said Lucy, "she's awake, and she's no more frightened than you are."

("You hear that," said Max to Brenda. "You take example by her, my dear!")

"But if we are going the wrong way, we shan't reach the Great Sloth," Lucy went on.

"Sooner or later, one way or another, we shall come to him," said the parrot, "and time is of no importance to a Great Sloth."

It was now very cold, and our travelers were glad to wrap themselves in the flags of all nations with which the yacht was handsomely provided. Philip made a sort of tabard of the Union Jack and the old Royal Arms of England, with the lilies and leopards; and Lucy wore the Japanese flag as a shawl. She said the picture of the sun on it made her feel warm. But Philip shivered under his complicated crosses and lions, as the *Lightning Loose* swept on over the dark tide between the dark walls and under the dark roof of the cavern.

"Cheer up," said the parrot. "Think what a lot of adventures you're having that no one else has ever had: think what a lot of things you'll have to tell the other boys when you go to school."

"The other boys wouldn't believe a word of it," said Philip in gloom. "I wouldn't unless I knew it was true."

"What I think is," said Lucy, watching the yellow light from the lamps rushing ahead along the roof, "that we shan't want to tell people. It'll be just enough to know it ourselves and talk about it, just Philip and me together."

"Well, as to that—" the parrot was beginning doubtfully, when he broke off to exclaim:

"Do my claws deceive me or is there a curious vibration, and noticeable acceleration of velocity?"

"Eh?" said Philip, which is not manners, and he knew it.

"He means," said Max stolidly, "aren't we going rather fast and rather wobbly?"

We certainly were. The *Lightning Loose* was going faster and faster along that subterranean channel, and every now and then gave a lurch and a shiver.

"Oh!" whined Brenda. "This is a dreadful place for dear little dogs!"

"Philip!" said Lucy in a low voice. "I know something is going to happen. Something dreadful. We *are* friends, aren't we?"

"Yes," said Philip firmly.

"Then I wish you'd kiss me."

"I can like you just as much without that," said Philip uneasily. "Kissing people—it's silly, don't you think?"

"Nobody's kissed me since Daddy went away," she said, "except Helen. And you don't mind kissing Helen. She *said* you were going to adopt me for your sister."

"Oh! All right," said Philip, and put his arm around her and kissed her. She felt so little and helpless and bony in his arm that he suddenly felt sorry for her, kissed her again more kindly and then, withdrawing his arm, thumped her hearteningly on the back.

"Be a man," he said in tones of comradeship and encouragement. "I'm perfectly certain nothing's going to happen. We're just going through a tunnel, and presently we shall just come out into the open air again, with the sky and the stars going on as usual."

He spoke this standing on the prow beside Lucy, and as he spoke she clutched his arm.

"Oh, look," she breathed, "oh, listen!"

He listened. And he heard a dull echoing roar that got louder and

166

*Plunged headlong over the edge*

louder. And he looked. The light of the lamps shone ahead on the dark gleaming water, and then quite suddenly it did not shine on the water because there was no longer any water for it to shine on. Only great empty black darkness. A great hole, ahead, into which the stream poured itself. And now they were at the edge of the gulf. The *Lightning Loose* gave a shudder and a bound and hung for what seemed a long moment on the edge of the precipice down which the underground river was pouring itself in a smooth sleek stream, rather like poured treacle, over what felt like the edge of everything solid.

The moment ended, and the little yacht, with Philip and Lucy and the parrot and the two dogs, plunged headlong over the edge into the dark unknown abyss below.

"It's all right, Lu," said Philip in that moment. "I'll take care of you."

And then there was silence in the cavern—only the rushing sound of the great waterfall echoed in the rocky arch.

CHAPTER TEN

# The Great Sloth

YOU HAVE heard of Indians shooting rapids in their birch-bark canoes? And perhaps you have yourself sailed a toy boat on a stream, and made a dam of clay, and waited with more or less patience till the water rose nearly to the top, and then broken a bit of your dam out and made a waterfall and let your boat drift over the edge of it. You know how it goes slowly at first, then hesitates and sweeps on more and more quickly. Sometimes it upsets, and sometimes it shudders and strains and trembles and sways to one side and to the other, and at last rights itself and makes up its mind, and rushes on down the stream, usually to be entangled in the clump of rushes at the stream's next turn. This is what happened to that good yacht, the *Lightning Loose*. She shot over the edge of that dark smooth subterranean waterfall, hung a long breathless moment between still air and falling water, slid down like a flash, dashed into the stream below, shuddered, reeled, righted herself, and sped on. You have perhaps been down the water chute at Earl's Court? It was rather like that.

"It's—it's all right," said Philip, in a rather shaky whisper. "She's going on all right."

"Yes," said Lucy, holding his arm very tight, "yes, I'm sure she's going on all right."

"Are we drowned?" said a trembling squeak. "Oh, Max, are we really drowned?"

"I don't think so," Max replied with caution. "And if we are, my dear, we cannot undrown ourselves by screams."

"Far from it," said the parrot, who had for the moment been rendered quite speechless by the shock. And you know a parrot is not made speechless just by any little thing. "So we may just as well try to behave," it said.

The lamps had certainly behaved, and behaved beautifully; through the wild air of the fall, the wild splash as the *Lightning Loose* struck the stream below, the lamps had shone on, seemingly undisturbed.

"An example to us all," said the parrot.

"Yes, but," said Lucy, "what are we to do?"

"When adventures take a turn one is far from expecting, one does what one can," said the parrot.

"And what's that?"

"Nothing," said the parrot. "Philip has relieved Max at the helm and is steering a straight course between the banks—if you can call them banks. There is nothing else to be done."

There plainly wasn't. The *Lightning Loose* rushed on through the darkness. Lucy reflected for a moment and then made cocoa. This was real heroism. It cheered everyone up, including the cocoa-maker herself. It was impossible to believe that anything dreadful was going to happen when you were making that soft, sweet, ordinary drink.

"I say," Philip remarked when she carried a cup to him at the wheel, "I've been thinking. All this is out of a book. Someone must have let it out. I know what book it's out of too. And if the whole story got out of the book we're all right. Only we shall go on for ages and climb out at last, three days' journey from Trieste."

"I see," said Lucy, and added that she hated geography. "Drink your cocoa while it's hot," she said in motherly accents, and, "what book is it?"

"It's *The Last Cruise of the Teal*," he said. "Helen gave it me just before she went away. It's a ripping book, and I used it for the roof of the outer court of the Hall of Justice. I remember it perfectly. The chaps on the *Teal* made torches of paper soaked in paraffin."

"We haven't any," said Lucy, "besides, our lamps light everything up all right. Oh! There's Brenda crying again. She hasn't a shadow of pluck."

She went quickly to the cabin where Max was trying to cheer Brenda by remarks full of solid good sense, to which Brenda paid no attention whatever.

"I knew how it would be," she kept saying in a whining voice, "I told you so from the beginning. I wish we hadn't come. I want to go home. Oh! What a dreadful thing to happen to dear little dogs."

"Brenda," said Lucy firmly, "if you don't stop whining you shan't have any cocoa."

Brenda stopped at once and wagged her tail appealingly.

"Cocoa?" she said. "Did anyone say cocoa? My nerves are so delicate. I know I'm a trial, dear Max, it's no use your pretending I'm not, but there is nothing like cocoa for the nerves. Plenty of sugar, please, dear Lucy. Thank you so much! Yes, it's *just* as I like it."

"There will be other things to eat by and by," said Lucy. "People who whine won't get any."

"I'm sure nobody would *dream* of whining," said Brenda. "I know I'm too sensitive, but you can do anything with dear little dogs by kindness. And as for whining—do you know, it's a thing I've never been subject to, from a child, never. Max will tell you the same."

Max said nothing, but only fixed his beautiful eyes hopefully on the cocoa jug.

And all the time the yacht was speeding along the underground stream, beneath the vast arch of the underground cavern.

"The worst of it is we may be going ever so far away from where we want to get to," said Philip, when Max had undertaken the steering again.

"All roads," remarked the parrot, "lead to Somnolentia. And besides, the ship is traveling due north—at least so the ship's compass states, and I have no reason as yet for doubting its word."

"Hullo!" cried more than one voice, and the ship shot out of the dark cavern into a sheet of water that lay spread under a white dome. The stream that had brought them there seemed to run across one side of this pool. Max, directed by the parrot, steered the ship into smooth water, where she lay at rest at last in the very middle of this great underground lake.

"*This* isn't out of *The Cruise of the Teal*," said Philip. "They must have shut that book."

"I think it's out of a book about Mexico or Peru or Ingots or some geographical place," said Lucy. "It had a green-and-gold binding. I think you used it for the other end of the outer justice court. And if you did, this dome's solid silver, and there's a hole in it, and under this dome there's untold treasure in gold incas."

"What's incas?"

"Gold bars, I believe," said Lucy. "And Mexicans come down through the hole in the roof and get it, and when enemies come they flood it with water. It's flooded now," she added unnecessarily.

"I wish adventures had never been invented," said Brenda. "No, dear Lucy, I am not whining. Far from it. But if a dear little dog might suggest it, we should all be better in a home, should we not?"

All eyes now perceived a dark hole in the roof, a round hole exactly in the middle of the shining dome. And as they gazed the dark hole became light. And they saw above them a white shining disk like a very large and very bright moon. It was the light of day.

"Someone has opened the trapdoor," said Lucy. "The Ingots always closed their treasure-vaults with trapdoors."

The bright disk was obscured; confused shapes broke its shining roundness. Then another disk, small and very black, appeared in the middle of it; the black disk grew larger and larger and larger. It was coming down to them. Slowly and steadily it came; now it reached the level of the dome, now it hung below it; down, down, down it came, past the level of their eager eyes, and splashed in the water close by the ship. It was a large empty bucket. The rope that held it was jerked from above; the bucket dipped and filled and was drawn up again slowly and steadily till it disappeared in the hole in the roof.

"Quick," said the parrot, "get the ship exactly under the hole, and next time the bucket comes down you can go up in it."

"This is out of the *Arabian Nights*, I think," said Lucy, when the yacht was directly under the hole in the roof. "But who is it that keeps on opening the books? Somebody must be pulling Polistopolis down."

"The Pretenderette, I shouldn't wonder," said Philip gloomily. "She isn't the Deliverer, so she must be the Destroyer. Nobody else can get into Polistarchia, you know."

"There's me."

"Oh, you're Deliverer too."

"Thank you," said Lucy gratefully. "But there's Helen."

"She was only on the Island, you know; she couldn't come to Polistarchia. Look out!"

The bucket was descending again, and instead of splashing in the water it bumped on the deck.

"You go first," said Philip to Lucy.

"And you," said Max to Brenda.

"Oh, I'll go first if you like," said Philip.

"Yes," said Max, "I'll go first if you like, Brenda."

You see Philip felt that he ought to give Lucy the first chance of escaping from the poor *Lightning Loose*. Yet he could not be at all sure what it was that she would be escaping to. And if there was danger overhead, of course he ought to be the one to go first to face it. And the worthy Max felt the same about Brenda.

And Lucy felt just the same as they did. I don't know what Brenda felt. She whined a little. Then for one moment Lucy and Philip stood on the deck, each grasping the handle of the bucket and looking at each other, and the dogs looked at them, and the parrot looked at everyone in turn. An impatient jerk and shake of the rope from above reminded them that there was no time to lose.

Lucy decided that it was more dangerous to go than to stay, just at the same moment when Philip decided that it was more dangerous to stay than to go, so when Lucy stepped into the bucket Philip helped her eagerly. Max thought the same as Philip, and I am afraid Brenda agreed with them. At any rate she leaped into Lucy's lap and curled her long length around just as the rope tightened and the bucket began to go up. Brenda screamed faintly, but her scream was stifled at once.

"I'll send the bucket down again the moment I get up," Lucy called out; and a moment later, "it feels awfully jolly, like a swing."

And so saying she was drawn up into the hole in the roof of the dome. Then a sound of voices came down the shaft, a confused sound; the anxious little party on the *Lightning Loose* could not make out any distinct words. They all stood staring up, expecting, waiting for the bucket to come down again.

"I hate leaving the ship," said Philip.

"You shall be the last to leave her," said the parrot consolingly, "that is if we can manage about Max without your having to sit on him in the bucket if he gets in first."

"But how about you?" said Philip.

A little arrogantly the parrot unfolded half a bright wing.

"Oh!" said Philip, enlightened and reminded. "Of course! And you might have flown away at any time. And yet you stuck to us. I say, you know, that was jolly decent of you."

"Not at all," said the parrot with conscious modesty.

"But it was," Philip insisted. "You might have—hullo!" cried Philip. The bucket came down again with a horrible rush. They held their breaths and looked to see the form of Lucy hurtling through the air. But no, the bucket swung loose a moment in midair, then it was hastily drawn up, and a hollow metallic clang echoed through the cavern.

174

*The bucket began to go up.*

"Brenda!" The cry was wrung from the heart of the sober self-contained Max.

"My wings and claws!" exclaimed the parrot.

"Oh, bother!" said Philip.

There was some excuse for these expressions of emotion. The white disk overhead had suddenly disappeared. Someone up above had banged the lid down. And all the manly hearts were below in the cave, and brave Lucy and helpless Brenda were above in a strange place, whose dangers those below could only imagine.

"I wish *I'd* gone," said Philip. "Oh, I *wish* I'd gone."

"Yes, indeed," said Max, with a deep sigh.

"I feel a little faint," said the parrot. "If someone would make a cup of cocoa."

Thus did the excellent bird seek to occupy their minds in that first moment of disaster. And it was well that the captain and crew were thus saved from despair. For before the kettle boiled, the lid of the shaft opened about a foot and something largeish, roundish, and lumpish fell heavily and bounced upon the deck of the *Lightning Loose*.

It was a pineapple, fresh, ripe, and juicy. On its side was carved in large letters of uncertain shape the one word "WAIT."

It was good advice and they took it. Really, I do not see what else they could have done in any case. And they ate the pineapple. And presently everyone felt extremely sleepy.

"Waiting is one of those things that you can do as well asleep as awake, or even better," said the parrot. "Forty winks will do us all the good in the world." He put his head under his wing where he sat on the binnacle.

"May I turn in alongside you, sir?" Max asked. "I shan't feel the dreadful loneliness so much then."

So Philip and Max curled up together on the deck, warmly covered with the spare flags of all nations, and the forty winks lasted for the space of a good night's rest—about ten hours, in fact. So ten hours' waiting was got through quite easily. But there was more waiting to do after they woke up, and that was not so easy.

When Lucy, sitting in the bucket with Brenda in her lap, felt the bucket lifted from the deck and swung loose in the air, it was as much as she could do to refrain from screaming. Brenda *did* scream, as you know, but Lucy stifled the sound in the folds of her frock.

Lucy bit her lips, made a great effort and called out that remark about the bucket-swing, just as though she were quite comfortable. It was very brave of her and helped her to go on being brave.

The bucket drew slowly up and up and up and passed from the silver dome into the dark shaft above. Lucy looked up. Yes, it was day-light that showed at the top of the shaft, and the rope was drawing her up toward it. Suppose the rope broke? Brenda was quite quiet now. She said afterward that she must have fainted. And now the light was nearer and nearer. Now Lucy was in it, for the bucket had been drawn right up, and hands were reached out to draw it over the side of what seemed like a well. At that moment Lucy saw in a flash what might happen if the owners of the hands, in their surprise, let go the bucket and the windlass. She caught Brenda in her hands and threw the dog out onto the dry ground, and threw herself across the well parapet. Just in time, for a shout of surprise went up and the bucket went down, clanging against the well sides. The hands *had* let go.

Lucy clambered over the well side slowly, and when her feet stood on firm ground she saw that the hands were winding up the bucket again, and that it came very easily.

"Oh, don't!" she said. "Let it go right down! There are some more people down there."

"Sorry, but it's against the rules. The bucket only goes down this well forty times a day. And that was the fortieth time."

They pulled the bucket in and banged down the lid of the well. Someone padlocked it and put the key in his pocket. And Lucy and he stood facing each other. He was a little round-headed man in a

*Lucy . . . threw herself across the well parapet.*

curious stiff red tunic, and there was something about the general shape of him and his tunic that reminded Lucy of something, only she could not remember what. Behind him stood two others, also red-tunicked and round-headed.

Brenda crouched at Lucy's feet and whined softly, and Lucy waited for the strangers to speak.

"You shouldn't do that," said the red-tunicked man at last. "It was a great shock to us, your bobbing up as you did. It will keep us awake at night, just remembering it."

"I'm sorry," said Lucy.

"You should always come into strange towns by the front gate," said the man. "Try to remember that, will you? Good night."

"But you're not going off like this," said Lucy. "Let me write a note and drop it down to the others. Have you a bit of pencil, and paper?"

"No," said the strange people, staring at her.

"Haven't you anything I can write on?" Lucy asked them.

"There's nothing here but pineapples," said one of them at last.

So she cut a pineapple from among the hundreds that grew among the rocks nearby, and carved "WAIT" on it with her penknife.

"Now," she said, "open that well lid."

"It's as much as our lives are worth," said the leader.

"No it isn't," said Lucy. "There's no law against dropping pine-apples into the well. You know there isn't. It isn't like drawing water. And if you don't I shall set my little dog at you. She is very fierce."

Brenda was so flattered that she showed her teeth and growled.

"Oh, very well," said the stranger, "anything to avoid fuss."

When the well lid was padlocked down again, Lucy said:

"What country is this?" though she was almost sure, because of the pineapples, that it was Somnolentia. And when they had said that word she said:

"Now I'll tell you something. The Deliverer is coming up that well next time you draw water. He is coming to deliver you from the bondage of the Great Sloth."

"It is true," said the red round-headed leader, "that we are in bondage. And the Great Sloth wearies us with the singing of choric songs when we long to be asleep. But none can deliver us. There is no hope. There is nothing good but sleep. And of that we have never enough."

"Oh, dear," said Lucy despairingly, "aren't there any women here? They always have more sense than men."

"What you say is rude as well as untrue," said the red leader, "but to avoid fuss we will lead you and your fierce dog to the huts of the women. And then perhaps you will allow us to go to sleep."

The huts were poor and mean, little fenced-in corners in the ruins of what had once been a great and beautiful city, with gardens and streams; but now the streams were dry and nothing grew in the gardens but weeds and pineapples.

But the women—who all wore green tunics of the same stiff shape as the men's—were not quite so sleepy as their husbands. They brought Lucy fresh pineapples to eat, and were dreamily interested in the cut of her clothes and the begging accomplishments of Brenda. And from the women she learned several things about the Somnolentians. They all wore the same shaped tunics, only the colors differed. The women's were green, the drawers of water wore red, the attendants of the Great Sloth wore black, and the pineapple gatherers wore yellow.

And as Lucy sat at the door of the hut and watched the people in these four colors going lazily about among the ruins she suddenly knew what they were, and she exclaimed:

"I know what you are; you're Halma men."

Instantly every man within earshot made haste to get away, and the women whispered, "Hush! It is death to breathe that name."

"But why?" Lucy asked.

"Halma was the great captain of our race," said the woman, "and the Great Sloth fears that if we hear his name it will rouse us and we shall break from bondage and become once more a free people."

Lucy determined that they should hear that name pretty often, but before she could speak it again the woman sighed, and remarking, "The Great Sloth sleeps," fell asleep then and there over the pineapple she was peeling. A vast silence settled on the city, and next moment Lucy also slept. She slept for hours.

It took her some time to find the keeper of the padlock key, and when she had found him he refused to use it. Nothing would move him, not even the threat of the fierceness of Brenda.

At last, almost in despair, Lucy suddenly remembered a word of power.

"I command you to open the well and let down the bucket," she said. "I command you by the great name of Halma."

"It is death to speak that name," said the keeper of the key, looking over his shoulder anxiously.

"It is life to speak that name," said Lucy. "Halma! Halma! Halma! If you don't open that well I'll carve the name on a pineapple and send it in on the golden tray with the Great Sloth's dinner."

"It would have the lives of hundreds for that," said the keeper in horror.

"Open the well, then," said Lucy.

They all held a council as soon as Philip and Max had been safely drawn up in the bucket, and Lucy told them all she knew.

"I think whatever we do we ought to be quick," said Lucy. "That Great Sloth is dangerous. I'm sure it is. It's sent already to say I am to be brought to its presence to sing songs to it while it goes to sleep. It doesn't mind me because it knows I'm not the Deliverer. And if you'll let me, I believe I can work everything all right. But if it knows you're here, it'll be much harder."

The degraded Halma men were watching them from a distance, in whispering groups.

"I shall go and sing to the Great Sloth," she said, "and you must go about and say the name of power to everyone you meet, and tell them you're the Deliverer. Then if my idea doesn't come off, we must overpower the Great Sloth by numbers and . . . You just go about saying 'Halma!'—see?"

"While you do the dangerous part? Likely!" said Philip.

"It's not dangerous. It never hurts the people who sing—never," said Lucy. "Now I'm going."

And she went before Philip could stop her.

"Let her go," said the parrot, "she is a wise child."

The temple of the Great Sloth was built of solid gold. It had beautiful pillars and doorways and windows and courts, one inside the other, each paved with gold flagstones. And in the very middle of everything was a large room that was entirely featherbed. There the Great Sloth passed its useless life in eating, sleeping, and listening to music.

Outside the moorish arch that led to this inner room Lucy stopped and began to sing. She had a clear little voice and she sang "Jockey to the Fair," and "Early One Morning," and then she stopped.

And a great sleepy slobbery voice came out from the room and said:

"Your songs are in very bad taste. Do you know no sleepy songs?"

"Your people sing you sleepy songs," said Lucy. "What a pity they can't sing to you all the time."

"You have a sympathetic nature," said the Great Sloth, and it came out and leaned on the pillar of its door and looked at her with sleepy interest. It was enormous, as big as a young elephant, and it walked on its hind legs like a gorilla. It was very black indeed.

"It *is* a pity," it said, "but they say they cannot live without drinking, so they waste their time in drawing water from the wells."

"Wouldn't it be nice," said Lucy, "if you had a machine for drawing water. Then they could sing to you all day—if they chose."

"If *I* chose," said the Great Sloth, yawning like a hippopotamus. "I am sleepy. Go!"

"No," said Lucy, and it was so long since the Great Sloth had heard that word that the shock of the sound almost killed its sleepiness.

"*What* did you say?" it asked, as if it could not believe its large ears.

"I said, 'No,'" said Lucy. "I mean that you are so great and grand you have only to wish for anything and you get it."

"Is that so?" said the Great Sloth dreamily and like an American.

"Yes," said Lucy with firmness. "You just say, 'I wish I had a machine to draw up water for eight hours a day.' That's the proper length for a working day. Father says so."

"Say it all again, and slower," said the creature. "I didn't quite catch what you said."

Lucy repeated the words.

"If that's all . . ." said the Great Sloth. "Now say it again, very slowly indeed."

Lucy did so and the Great Sloth repeated after her:

"I wish I had a machine to draw up water for eight hours a day."

"Don't," it said angrily, looking back over its shoulder into the feather-bedded room. "Don't, I say. Where are you shoving to? Who are you? What are you doing in my room? Come out of it."

Something did come out of the room, pushing the Great Sloth away from the door. And what came out was the vast featherbed in enormous rolls and swellings and bulges. It was being pushed out by something so big and strong that it was stronger that the Great Sloth itself, and pushed that mountain of lazy sloth-flesh half across its own inner courtyard. Lucy retreated before its advancing bulk and its extreme rage.

"Push me out of my own feather bedroom, would it?" said the Sloth, now hardly sleepy at all. "You wait till I get hold of it, whatever it is."

The whole of the featherbed was out in the courtyard now, and the Great Sloth climbed slowly back over it into its room to find out who had dared to outrage its Slothful Majesty.

Lucy waited, breathless with hope and fear, as the Great Sloth blundered back into the inner room of its temple. It did not come out again. There was a silence, and then a creaking sound and the voice of the Great Sloth saying:

"No, no, no, I won't. Let go, I tell you." Then more sounds of creaking and the sound of metal on metal.

She crept to the arch and peeped around it.

The room that had been full of featherbed was now full of wheels and cogs and bands and screws and bars. It was full, in fact, of a large and complicated machine. And the handle of that machine was being turned by the Great Sloth itself.

"Let me go," said the Great Sloth, gnashing its great teeth. "I won't work!"

"You must," said a purring voice from the heart of the machinery. "You wished for me, and now you have to work me eight hours a day. It is the law." It was the machine itself which spoke.

"I'll break you," said the Sloth.

"I am unbreakable," said the machine with gentle pride.

"This is your doing," said the Sloth, turning its furious eyes on Lucy in the doorway. "You wait till I catch you!" And all the while it had to go on turning that handle.

"Thank you," said Lucy politely. "I think I will not wait. And I shall have eight hours' start," she added.

Even as she spoke a stream of clear water began to run from the pumping machine. It slid down the gold steps and across the golden court. Lucy ran out into the ruined square of the city shouting:

"Halma! Halma! Halma! To me, Halma's men!"

And the men, already excited by Philip, who had gone about saying that name of power without a moment's pause all the time Lucy had been in the golden temple, gathered around her in a crowd.

"Quick!" she said. "The Great Sloth is pumping water up for you. He will pump for eight hours a day. Quick! Dig a channel for the water to run in. The Deliverer," she pointed to Philip, "has given you back your river."

*And all the while it had to go on turning that handle.*

Some ran to look out old rusty half-forgotten spades and picks. But others hesitated and said:

"The Great Sloth will work for eight hours, and then it will be free to work vengeance on us."

"I will go back," said Lucy, "and explain to it that if it does not behave nicely you will all wish for machine guns, and it knows now that if people wish for machinery they have to use it. It will be awake now for eight hours and if you all work for eight hours a day you'll soon have your city as fine as ever. And there's one new law. Every time the clock strikes you must all say 'Halma!' aloud, every one of you, to remind yourselves of your great destiny, and that you are no longer slaves of the Great Sloth."

She went back and explained machine guns very carefully to the now hardworking Sloth. When she came back all the men were at work digging a channel for the new river.

The women and children crowded round Lucy and Philip.

"Ah!" said the oldest woman of all. "Now we shall be able to wash in water. I've heard my grandmother say water was very pleasant to wash in. I never thought I should live to wash in water myself."

"Why?" Lucy asked. "What do you wash in?"

"Pineapple juice," said a dozen voices, "when we *do* wash!"

"But that must be very sticky," said Lucy.

"It is," said the oldest woman of all, "very!"

CHAPTER ELEVEN

# The Night Attack

THE HALMA men were not naturally lazy. They were, in the days before the coming of the Great Sloth, a most energetic and industrious people. Now that the Sloth was obliged to work eight hours a day, the weight of its constant and catching sleepiness was taken away, and the people set to work in good earnest. (I did explain, didn't I, that the Great Sloth's sleepiness really was catching, like measles?)

So now the Halma men were as busy as ants. Some dug the channel for the new stream, some set to work to restore the buildings, while others weeded the overgrown gardens and plowed the deserted fields. The head Halma man painted in large letters on a column in the marketplace these words:

"This city is now called by its ancient name of Briskford. Any citizen found calling it Somnolentia will not be allowed to wash in water for a week."

The headman was full of schemes, the least of which was the lighting of the town by electricity, the power to be supplied by the Great Sloth.

"He can't go on pumping eight hours a day," said the head-man. "I can easily adjust the machine to all sorts of other uses."

In the evening a banquet was (of course) given to the Deliverers. The banquet was all pineapple and water, because there had been no time to make or get anything else. But the speeches were very flattering, and Philip and Lucy were very pleased, more so than Brenda, who did not like pineapple and made but little effort to conceal her disappointment. Max accepted bits of pineapple, out of politeness, and hid them among the feet of the guests so that nobody's feelings should be hurt.

"I don't know how we're to get back to the island," said Philip next day, "now we've lost the *Lightning Loose.*"

"I think we'd better go back by way of Polistopolis," said Lucy, "and find out who's been opening the books. If they go on they may let simply anything out. And if the worst comes to the worst, perhaps we could get someone to help us to open the *Teal* book again and get the *Teal* out to cross to the island in."

"Lu," said Philip with feeling, "you're clever, really clever. No, I'm not kidding. I mean it. And I'm sorry I ever said you were only a girl. But how are we to get to Polistopolis?"

It was a difficult problem. The headman could offer no suggestions. It was Brenda who suggested asking the advice of the Great Sloth.

"He is such a fine figure of an animal," she said admiringly, "so handsome and distinguished-looking. I am sure he must have a really great mind. I always think good looks go with really great minds, don't you, dear Lucy?"

"We might as well," said Philip, "if no one can think of anything else."

No one could. So they decided to take Brenda's advice.

Now that the Sloth worked every day it was not nearly so disagreeable as it had been when it slept so much.

The children approached it at the dinner hour and it listened patiently if drowsily to their question. When it had quite done, it reflected—or seemed to reflect; perhaps it had fallen asleep—until the town clock struck one, the time for resuming work. Then it got up and slouched toward its machine.

"Cucumbers," it said, and began to turn the handle of its wheel. They had to wait till teatime to ask it what it meant, for in that town the rule about not speaking to the man at the wheel was strictly enforced.

"Cucumbers," the Sloth repeated, and added a careful explanation. "You sit on the end of any young cucumber which points in the desired direction, and when it has grown to its full length—say sixteen inches—why, then you are sixteen inches on your way."

"But that's not much," said Lucy.

"Every little helps," said the Sloth, "more haste less speed. Then you wait till the cucumber seeds, and, when the new plants grow, you select the earliest cucumber that points in the desired direction and take your seat on it. By the end of the cucumber season you will be another sixteen—or with luck seventeen—inches on your way. Thirty-two inches in all, almost a yard. And thus you progress toward your goal, slowly but surely, like in politics."

"Thank you very much," said Philip, "we will think it over."

But it did not need much thought.

"If we could get a motorcar!" said Philip. "If you can get machines by wishing for them . . ."

"The very thing," said Lucy. "Let's find the headman. *We* mustn't wish for a motor or we should have to go on using it. But perhaps there's someone here who'd like to drive a motor—for his living, you know?"

There was. A Halma man, with an inborn taste for machinery, had long pined to leave the gathering of pineapples to others. He was induced to wish for a motor and a B.S.A. sixty horsepower car snorted suddenly in the place where a moment before no car was.

"Oh, the luxury! This is indeed like home," sighed Brenda, curling up on the air cushions.

And the children certainly felt a gloriously restful sensation. Nothing to be done; no need to think or bother. Just to sit quiet and be borne swiftly on through wonderful cities, all of which Philip vaguely remembered to have seen, small and near, and built by his own hands and Helen's.

And so, at last, they came close to Polistopolis. Philip never could tell how it was that he stopped the car outside the city. It must have been some quite unaccountable instinct, because naturally, you know, when you are not used to being driven in motors, you like to dash up to the house you are going to, and enjoy your friends' enjoyment of the grand way in which you have traveled. But Philip felt—in that quite certain and quite unexplainable way in which you do feel things sometimes—that it was best to stop the car among the suburban groves of southernwood, and to creep into the town in the disguise afforded by motor coats, motor veils, and motor goggles. (For, of course, all these had come with the motorcar when it was wished for, because no motorcar is complete without them.)

They said good-bye warmly to the Halma motor man, and went quietly toward the town, Max and Brenda keeping to heel in the most praiseworthy way, and the parrot nestling inside Philip's jacket, for it was chilled by the long rush through the evening air.

And now the scattered houses and spacious gardens gave place to the streets of Polistopolis, the capital of the kingdom. And the streets were strangely deserted. The children both felt—in that quite certain and unexplainable way—that it would be unwise of them to go to the place where they had slept the last time they were in that city.

The whole party was very tired. Max walked with drooping tail, and Brenda was whining softly to herself from sheer weariness and weak-mindedness. The parrot alone was happy—or at least contented. Because it was asleep.

At the corner of a little square planted with southernwood trees in tubs, Philip called a halt.

"Where shall we go?" he said. "Let us put it to the vote."

*Philip felt . . . that it was best to stop the car among*
*the suburban groves of southernwood.*

And even as he spoke, he saw a dark form creeping along in the shadow of the houses.

"Who goes there?" Philip cried with proper spirit, and the answer surprised him, all the more that it was given with a kind of desperate bravado.

"I go here; I, Plumbeus, Captain of the old Guard of Polistopolis."

"Oh, it's you!" cried Philip. "I *am* glad. You can advise us. Where can we go to sleep? Somehow or other I don't care to go to the house where we stayed before."

The captain made no answer. He simply caught at the hands of Lucy and Philip, dragged them through a low, arched doorway, and, as soon as the long lengths of Brenda and Max had slipped through, closed the door.

"Safe," he said in a breathless way, which made Philip feel that safety was the last thing one could count on at that moment.

"Now, speak low, who knows what spies may be listening? I am a plain man. I speak as I think. You came out of the unknown. You may be the Deliverer or the Destroyer. But I am a judge of faces—always was from a boy—and I cannot believe that this countenance of apple-cheeked innocence is that of a Destroyer."

Philip was angry and Lucy was furious. So he said nothing. And she said:

"Apple-cheeked yourself!" which was very rude.

"I see that you are annoyed," said the captain in the dark, where, of course, he could see nothing, "but in calling your friend apple-cheeked I was merely offering the highest compliment in my power. The absence of fruit in this city is, I suppose, the reason why our compliments are like that. I believe poets say 'sweet as a rose'—*we* say 'sweet as an orange.' May I be allowed unreservedly to apologize?"

"Oh, that's all right," said Philip awkwardly.

"And to ask whether you *are* the Deliverer?"

"I hope so," said Philip modestly.

"Of course he is," said the parrot, putting its head out from the

192

front of Philip's jacket, "and he has done six deeds out of the seven already."

"It is time that deeds were done here," said the captain. "I'll make a light and get you some supper. I'm in hiding here; but the walls are thick and all the shutters are shut."

He bolted a door and opened the slide of a dark lantern.

"Some of us have taken refuge in the old prison," he said. "It's never used, you know, so her spies don't infest it as they do every other part of the city."

"Whose spies?"

"The Destroyer's," said the captain, getting bread and milk out of a cupboard. "At least, if you're the Deliverer she must be that. But she says she's the Deliverer."

He lighted candles and set them on the table as Lucy asked eagerly:

"What Destroyer? Is it a horrid woman in a motor veil?"

"You've guessed it," said the captain gloomily.

"It's that Pretenderette," said Philip. "Does Mr. Noah know? What has she been doing?"

"Everything you can think of," said the captain. "She says she's queen, and that she's done the seven deeds. And Mr. Noah doesn't know, because she's set a guard around the city, and no message can get out or in."

"The Hippogriff?" said Lucy.

"Yes, of course I thought of that," said the captain. "And so did she. She's locked it up and thrown the key into one of the municipal wells."

"But why do the guards obey her?" Philip asked.

"They're not *our* guards, of course," the captain answered. "They're strange soldiers that she got out of a book. She got the people to pull down the Hall of Justice by pretending there was fruit in the gigantic books it's built with. And when the book was opened these soldiers came marching out. The Sequani and the Aedui, they call themselves. And when you've finished supper we ought to hold a council. There are a lot of us here. All sorts. Distinctions of rank are forgotten in times of public peril."

Some twenty or thirty people presently gathered in that round room from whose windows Philip and Lucy had looked out when they were first imprisoned. There were indeed all sorts, match servants, domino men, soldiers, china men, Mr. Noah's three sons and his wife, a pirate, and a couple of sailors.

"What book," Philip asked Lucy in an undertone, "did she get these soldiers out of?"

"Caesar, I think," said Lucy. "And I'm afraid it was my fault. I remember telling her about the barbarians and the legions and things after father had told me—when she was my nurse, you know. She's very clever at thinking of horrid things to do, isn't she?"

The council talked for two hours, and nobody said anything worth mentioning. When everyone was quite tired out, everyone went to bed.

It was Philip who woke in the night in the grasp of a sudden idea.

"What is it?" asked Max, rousing himself from his warm bed at Philip's feet.

"I've thought of something," said Philip in a low excited voice. "I'm going to have a night attack."

"Shall I wake the others?" asked Max, ever ready to oblige.

Philip thought a moment. Then:

"No," he said, "it's rather dangerous, and besides, I want to do it all by myself. Lucy's done more than her share already. Look out, Max; I'm going to get up and go out."

He got up and he went out. There was a faint grayness of dawn now that showed him the great square of the city on which he and Lucy had looked from the prison window, a very long time ago as it seemed. He found without difficulty the ruins of the Hall of Justice.

And among the vast blocks scattered on the ground was one that seemed of gray marble, and bore on its back in gigantic letters of gold the words *De Bello Gallico*.

Philip stole back to the prison and roused the captain.

"I want twenty picked men," he said, "without boots—and at once."

He got them, and he led them to the ruins of the Justice Hall.

"Now," he said, "raise the cover of this book; only the cover, not any of the pages."

The men set their shoulders to the marble slab that was the book's cover and heaved it up. And as it rose on their shoulders Philip spoke softly, urgently.

"Caesar," he said, "Caesar!"

And a voice answered from under the marble slab.

"Who calls?" it said. "Who calls upon Julius Caesar?"

And from the space below the slab, as it were from a marble tomb, a thin figure stepped out, clothed in toga and cloak and wearing on its head a crown of bays.

"*I* called," said Philip in a voice that trembled a little. "There's no one but you who can help. The barbarians of Gaul hold this city. I call on great Caesar to drive them away. No one else can help us."

Caesar stood for a moment, silent in the gray twilight. Then he spoke.

"I will do it," he said. "You have often tried to master Caesar and always failed. Now you shall be no more ashamed of that failure, for you shall see Caesar's power. Bid your slaves raise the leaves of my book to the number of fifteen."

It was done, and Caesar turned toward the enormous open book.

"Come forth!" he said. "Come forth, my legions!"

Then something in the book moved suddenly, and out of it, as out of an open marble tomb, came long lines of silent armed men, ranged themselves in ranks, and, passing Caesar, saluted. And still more came, and more and more, each with the round shield and the shining helmet and the javelins and the terrible short sword. And on their backs were the packages they used to carry with them into war.

"The Barbarians of Gaul are loose in this city," said the voice of the great commander. "Drive them before you once more as you drove them of old."

"Whither, O Caesar?" asked one of the Roman generals.

"Drive them, O Titus Labienus," said Caesar, "back into that book wherein I set them more than nineteen hundred years ago, and from which they have dared to escape. Who is their leader?" he asked of Philip.

"The Pretenderette," said Philip, "a woman in a motor veil."

"Caesar does not war with women," said the man in the laurel crown. "Let her be taken prisoner and brought before me."

Low-voiced, the generals of Caesar's army gave their commands, and with incredible quietness the army moved away, spreading itself out in all directions.

"She has caged the Hippogriff," said Philip, "the winged horse, and we want to send him with a message."

"See that the beast is freed," said Caesar, and turned to Plumbeus the captain. "We be soldiers together," he said. "Lead me to the main gate. It is there that the fight will be fiercest." He laid a hand on the captain's shoulder, and at the head of the last legion, Caesar and the captain of the soldiers marched to the main gate.

# CHAPTER TWELVE

# The End

PHILIP TORE back to the prison, to be met at the door by Lucy.

"I hate you," she said briefly, and Philip understood.

"I couldn't help it," he said. "I did want to do something by myself."

And Lucy understood.

"And besides," he said, "I was coming back for you. Don't be snarky about it, Lu. I've called up Caesar himself. And you shall see him before he goes back into the book. Come on; if we're sharp we can hide in the ruins of the Justice Hall and see everything. I noticed there was a bit of the gallery left standing. Come on. I want you to think what message to send by the Hippogriff to Mr. Noah."

"Oh, you needn't trouble about that," said Lucy in an offhand manner. "I sent the parrot off *ages* ago."

"And you never told me! Then I think that's quits, don't you?"

Lucy had a short struggle with herself (you know those unpleasant and difficult struggles, I am sure!) and said:

"Right-o!"

And together they ran back to the Justice Hall.

The light was growing every moment, and there was now a sound of movement in the city. Women came down to the public fountains to draw water, and boys swept the paths and doorsteps. That sort of work goes on even when barbarians are surrounding a town. And the ordinary sounds of a town's awakening came to Lucy and Philip as they waited: crowing cocks and barking dogs and cats mewing faintly for the morning milk. But it was not for those sounds that Lucy and Philip were waiting.

So through those homely and familiar sounds they listened, listened, listened; and very gradually, so that they could neither of them have said at any moment, "Now it has begun," yet quite beyond mistake the sound for which they listened was presently loud in their ears. And it was the sound of steel on steel; the sound of men shouting in the breathless moment between sword stroke and sword stroke; the cry of victory and the wail of defeat.

And, presently, the sound of feet that ran.

And now a man shot out from a side street and ran across the square toward the Palace of Justice, where Lucy and Philip were hidden in the gallery. And now another and another all running hard and making for the ruined hall as hunted creatures make for cover. Rough, big, blond, their long hair flying behind them, and their tunics of beast skins flapping as they ran, the barbarians fled before the legions of Caesar. The great marble-covered book that looked like a marble tomb was still open, its cover and fifteen leaves propped up against the tall broken columns of the gateway of the Justice Hall. Into that open book leaped the first barbarian, leaped and vanished, and the next after him and the next, and then, by twos and threes and sixes and sevens, they leaped in and disappeared, amid gasping and shouting and the nearing sound of the bucina and of the trumpets of Rome.

Then from all quarters of the city the Roman soldiers came trooping, and as the last of the barbarians plunged headlong into the open book, the Romans formed into ordered lines and waited, while a man

*They leaped in and disappeared.*

might count ten. Then, advancing between their ranks, came the spare form and thin face of the man with the laurel crown.

Twelve thousand swords flashed in air and wavered a little like reeds in the breeze, then steadied themselves, and the shout went up from twelve thousand throats:

"Ave Caesar!"

And without haste and without delay the Romans filed through the ruins to the marble-covered book, and two by two entered it and disappeared. Each as he passed the mighty conqueror saluted him with proud mute reverence.

When the last soldier was hidden in the book, Caesar looked around him, a little wistfully.

"I must speak to him; I must," Lucy cried, "I *must*. Oh, what a darling he is!"

She ran down the steps from the gallery and straight to Caesar. He smiled when she reached him, and gently pinched her ear. Fancy going through the rest of your life hearing all the voices of the world through an ear that has been pinched by Caesar!

"Oh, thank you! Thank you!" said Philip. "How splendid you are. I'll swot up my Latin like anything next term, so as to read about you."

"Are they all in?" Lucy asked. "I do hope nobody was hurt."

Caesar smiled.

"A most unreasonable wish, my child, after a great battle!" he said. "But for once the unreasonable is the inevitable. Nobody was hurt. You see it was necessary to get every man back into the book just as he left it, or what would the schoolmasters have done? There remain now only my own guard who have in charge the false woman who let loose the barbarians. And here they come."

Surrounded by a guard with drawn swords the Pretenderette advanced slowly.

"Hail, woman!" said Caesar.

"Hail, whoever you are!" said the Pretenderette very sulkily.

"I hail," said Caesar, "your courage."

Philip and Lucy looked at each other. Yes, the Pretenderette had courage: they had not thought of that before. All the attempts she had made against them—she alone in a strange land—yes, these needed courage.

"And I demand to know how you came here."

"When I found he'd been at his building again," she said, pointing a contemptuous thumb at Philip, "I was just going to pull it down, and I knocked down a brick or two with my sleeve, and not thinking what I was doing I built them up again; and then I got a bit giddy and the whole thing seemed to begin to grow—candlesticks and bricks and dominoes and everything, bigger and bigger and bigger, and I looked in. It was as big as a church by this time, and I saw that boy losing his way among the candlestick pillars, and I followed him and I listened. And I thought I could be as good a Deliverer as anybody else. And the motor veil that I was going to catch the two thirty-seven train in was a fine disguise."

"You tried to injure the children," Caesar reminded her.

"I don't want to say anything to make you let me off," said the Pretenderette, "but at the beginning I didn't think any of it was real. I thought it was a dream. You can let your evil passions go in a dream and it don't hurt anyone."

"It hurts you," Caesar said.

"Oh! That's no odds," said the Pretenderette scornfully.

"You sought to injure and confound the children at every turn," said Caesar, "even when you found that things were real."

"I saw there was a chance of being Queen," said the Pretenderette, "and I took it. Seems to me you've no occasion to talk if you're Julius Caesar, the same as the bust in the library. You took what you could get right enough in your time, when all's said and done."

"I hail," said Caesar again, "your courage."

"You needn't trouble," she said, tossing her head, "my game's up now, and I'll speak my mind if I die for it. You don't understand.

You've never been a servant, to see other people get all the fat and you all the bones. What you think it's like to know if you'd just been born in a gentleman's mansion instead of in a model workman's dwelling you'd have been brought up as a young lady and had the openwork silk stockings and the lace on your under-petticoats."

"You go too deep for me," said Caesar, with the ghost of a smile. "I now pronounce your sentence. But life has pronounced on you a sentence worse than any I can give you. Nobody loves you."

"Oh, you old silly," said the Pretenderette in a burst of angry tears, "don't you see that's just why everything's happened?"

"You are condemned," said Caesar calmly, "to make yourself beloved. You will be taken to Briskford, where you will teach the Great Sloth to like his work and keep him awake for eight play-hours a day. In the intervals of your toil you must try to get fond of someone. The Halma people are kind and gentle. You will not find them hard to love. And when the Great Sloth loves his work and the Halma people are so fond of you that they feel they cannot bear to lose you, your penance will be over and you can go where you will."

"You know well enough," said the Pretenderette, still tearful and furious, "that if that ever happened I shouldn't want to go anywhere else."

"Yes," said Caesar slowly, "I know."

Lucy would have liked to kiss the Pretenderette and say she was sorry, but you can't do that when it is all other people's fault and *they* aren't sorry. And besides, before all these people, it would have looked like showing off. You know, I am sure, exactly how Lucy felt.

The Pretenderette was led away. And now Caesar stood facing the children, his hands held out in farewell. The growing light of early morning transfigured his face, and to Philip it suddenly seemed to be most remarkably like the face of That Man, Mr. Peter Graham, whom Helen had married. He was just telling himself not to be a duffer when Lucy cried out in a loud cracked-sounding voice, "Daddy, oh, Daddy!" and sprang forward.

And at that moment the sun rose above the city wall, and its rays gleamed redly on the helmet and the breastplate and the shield and the sword of Caesar. The light struck at the children's eyes like a blow. Dazzled, they closed their eyes and when they opened them, blinking and confused, Caesar was gone and the marble book was closed— forever.

Three days later Mr. Noah arrived by elephant, and the meeting between him and the children is, as they say, better imagined than described. Especially as there is not much time left now for describing anything. Mr. Noah explained that the freeing of Polistopolis from the Pretenderette and the barbarians counted as the seventh deed and that Philip had now attained the rank of King, the deed of the Great Sloth having given him the title of Prince of Pineapples. His expression of gratitude and admiration was of the warmest, and Philip felt that it was rather ungrateful of him to say, as he couldn't help saying:

"Now I've done all the deeds, mayn't I go back to Helen?"

"All in good time," said Mr. Noah. "I will at once set about the arrangements for your coronation."

The coronation was an occasion of unexampled splendor. There was a banquet (of course) and fireworks, and all the guns fired salutes and the soldiers presented arms, and the ladies presented bouquets. And at the end Mr. Noah, with a few well-chosen words that brought tears to all eyes, placed the gold crown of Polistarchia upon the brow of Philip, where its diamonds and rubies shone dazzlingly.

There was an extra crown for Lucy, made of silver and pearls and pale silvery moonstones.

You have no idea how the Polistarchians shouted.

"And now," said Mr. Noah when it was all over, "I regret to inform you that we must part. Polistarchia is a Republic, and of course in a republic kings and queens are not permitted to exist. Partings are painful things. And you had better go at once."

He was plainly very much upset.

"This is very sudden," said Philip.

And Lucy said, "I do think it's silly. How shall we get home? All in a hurry, like this?"

"How did you get here?"

"By building a house and getting into it."

"Then build your own house. Oh, we have models of all the houses you were ever in. The pieces are all numbered. You only have to put them together."

He led them to a large room behind the hall of Public Amusements and took down from a shelf a stout box labeled "The Grange." On another box Philip saw "Laburnum Cottage."

Mr. Noah, kneeling on his yellow mat, tumbled the contents of the box out on the floor, and Philip and Lucy set to work to build a house with the exquisitely finished little blocks and stones and beams and windows and chimneys.

"I cannot bear to see you go," said Mr. Noah. "Good-bye, good-bye. Remember me sometimes!"

"We shall never forget you," said the children, jumping up hugging him.

"Good-bye!" said the parrot who had followed them in.

"Good-bye, good-bye!" said everybody.

"I wish the *Lightning Loose* was not lost," Philip even at this parting moment remembered to say.

"She isn't," said Mr. Noah. "She flew back to the island directly you left her. Sails are called wings, are they not? White wings that never grow weary, you know. Relieved of your weight, the faithful yacht flew home like any pigeon."

"Hooray!" said Philip. "I couldn't bear to think of her rotting away in a cavern."

"I wish Max and Brenda had come to say good-bye," said Lucy.

"It is not needed," said Mr. Noah mysteriously. And then everybody said good-bye again, and Mr. Noah rolled up his yellow mat, put it under his arm again, and went—forever.

The children built the Grange, and when the beautiful little model of that house was there before them, perfect, they stood still a moment, looking at it.

"I wish we could be two people each," said Lucy, "and one of each of us go home and one of each of us stay here. Oh!" she cried suddenly, and snatched at Philip's arm. For a slight strange giddiness had suddenly caught her. Philip too swayed a little uncertainly and stood a moment with his hand to his head. The children gazed about them bewildered and still a little giddy. The room was gone, the model of the Grange was gone. Over their heads was blue sky, under their feet was green grass, and in front stood the Grange itself, with its front door wide open and on the steps Helen and Mr. Peter Graham.

That telegram had brought them home.

You will wonder how Lucy explained where she had been when she was lost. She never did explain. There are some things, as you know, that cannot be explained. But the curious thing is that no one ever asked for an explanation. The grown-ups must have thought they knew all about it, which, of course, was very far from being the truth.

When the four people on the doorstep of the Grange had finished saying how glad they were to see each other—that day on the steps when Philip and Lucy came back from Polistarchia, Helen and Mr. Peter Graham came back from Belgium—Helen said:

"And we've brought you each the loveliest present. Fetch them, Peter, there's a dear."

Mr. Peter Graham went to the stableyard and came back followed by two long tan dachshunds, who rushed up to the children frisking and fawning in a way they well knew.

"Why, Max! Why, Brenda!" cried Philip. "Oh, Helen! Are they for us?"

"Yes, dear, of course they are," said Helen, "but how did you know their names?"

That was one of the things which Philip could not tell, then.

But he told Helen the whole story later, and she said it was wonderful, and how clever of him to make all that up, and that when he was a man he would be able to be an author and to write books.

"And do you know," she said, "I *did* dream about the island—quite a long dream, only when I woke up I could only remember that I'd been there and seen you. But no doubt I dreamed about Mr. Noah and all the rest of it as well, only I forgot it."

And Max and Brenda of course loved everyone. Their characters were quite unchanged. Only the children had forgotten the language of animals, so that conversation between them and the dogs was forever impossible. But Max and Brenda understand every word you say—anyone can see that.

You want to know what became of the redheaded, steely-eyed nurse, the Pretenderette, who made so much mischief and trouble? Well, I suppose she is still living with the Halma folk, teaching the Great Sloth to like his work and learning to be fond of people—which is the only way to be happy. At any rate no one that I know of has ever seen her again anywhere else.

❖ *The End* ❖

# Afterword

BUILDING HOUSES, castles, and even cities out of household and decorative items is a common childhood activity. And what child hasn't imagined that his or her creation—or a doll or toy, for that matter—could come to life, especially when no one else is looking? Within the pages of her classic, *The Magic City*, E. Nesbit ingeniously invents a world that combines the reality of childhood play with the fantasy of childhood dreams, and brings it vividly to life for her readers.

The youngest of four children, Edith Nesbit was born in a rural suburb of London in 1858. She spent much of her youth in boarding schools and always loved to read and write stories and poems. From the age of fifteen, when her first poems were published, Nesbit earned money to help support her family by writing verse, short stories, and novels. She wrote under the name of E. Nesbit, and was pleased that many readers mistakenly assumed she was a man. Although she was successful in getting many of her works published, none achieved great critical acclaim until her tales of adventure and magic for children.

The year 1899 marked the publication of Nesbit's first major book for young readers, *The Story of the Treasure Seekers*. The unusually realistic behavior of the children in the story—their quarrels and reconcilia-tions, as well as their banding together in times of trouble—are easily recognizable experiences, even now, more than a century later. And readers today continue to be delighted by the novel's humorous blend of adventure and family life. The following year, Nesbit issued a marvelous collection of short stories, *The Book of Dragons,* which revealed her deft touch for creating tales of magic and fantasy. Then two years later, Nesbit transformed the world of children's literature with *Five Children and It*—the first of her refreshingly original fantasy/ adventure novels.

Before *Five Children and It* was published, two basic types of children's novels in this genre were predominant: in them, children usually traveled to some far-off fantasy kingdom (Alice to Wonderland, Dorothy to Oz); or else the story took place in a fairy-tale world completely independent from our own (as in George MacDonald's *At the Back of the North Wind*). In Nesbit's books, however, readers met children much like themselves, whose lives and problems seemed quite familiar. It was into this everyday setting that Nesbit introduced her singular brand of unpredictable magic.

Nesbit also wasn't afraid to address life's realities in her work. As a young girl, Nesbit had lost her father and seen her family's fortunes rise and fall, so she knew the pain and turmoil that sudden upheaval could bring to a child's world. In no book does she explore this idea more brilliantly than in *The Magic City,* first published in 1910.

In this story, Philip Haldane's happy existence as—in his mind—the sole man in his beloved sister's life is suddenly turned upside down when she marries; throwing him helter-skelter into a new home, com-plete with a new family, and—worst of all—a stepsister. Philip's resentment of all this upheaval is as recognizable today, in our world of frequent divorce and remarriage, as it was in Edwardian Britain. Although filled with magical creations, heroic deeds, and an urgent quest, *The Magic City* is first and foremost about Philip's personal journey to accept the changes that have been forced upon him—and to discover that his sister's love for her new husband in no way diminishes her love for him.

Traveling with Philip as he evolves from a hurt and angry child to a loving friend and brother is all the more exciting and moving because at some point in our lives—for one reason or another—we have all had to make a similar journey. And that is why, ninety years after its original publication, *The Magic City* continues to captivate, entertain, and touch our hearts.

—*Peter Glassman*

# E[DITH] NESBIT (1858–1924)

lived in England and had dreamed of becoming a poet since she was fifteen years old. After she married and her husband fell ill, it was up to Nesbit to support her small family. For the next nineteen years, she published a number of novels, essays, articles, poems, and short stories. But it was not until 1899 that *The Story of the Treasure Seekers*—the book that launched her career as a children's author—was published. Nesbit's groundbreaking style quickly gained a popularity that has lasted for more than a century. Her many books for young readers include *The Railway Children, Five Children and It,* and *The Enchanted Castle.*

# H[AROLD] R[OBERT] MILLAR (1891–1935)

lived in England and intended to study engineering, but abandoned it in favor of art. He illustrated numerous books for children, including nearly all of E. Nesbit's beloved fantasies as well as *The Golden Fairy Book,* by George Sands.

# PAUL O. ZELINSKY (jacket artist)

is the illustrator of many books for children, including *Rapunzel,* winner of the Caldecott Award, as well as *Hansel and Gretel, Rumplestiltskin,* and *Swamp Angel,* all Caldecott Honor Books. He lives with his family in Brooklyn, New York.

# PETER GLASSMAN

is the owner of Books of Wonder, the New York City bookstore specializing in both new and old imaginative books for children.